The world is ours.

The Greencloaks are too trusting. Go now, hide within them, and strike when the time is right.

Claim your spirit animal and join the adventure now:

1. Go to scholastic.com/spiritanimals.

2. Log in to create your character and choose your own spirit animal.

3. Have your book ready and enter the code below to unlock the adventure.

Your code:

NRPTFMC7MK

Gerathon demands it.

The Conquerors

scholastic.com/spiritanimals

The Greencloaks have
ignored your plight. They left
your people to suffer while
they silently took over the
rest of the world.

THE BOOK OF SHANE

Nick Eliopulos

INTRODUCTION BY

Tui T. Sutherland

SCHOLASTIC INC.

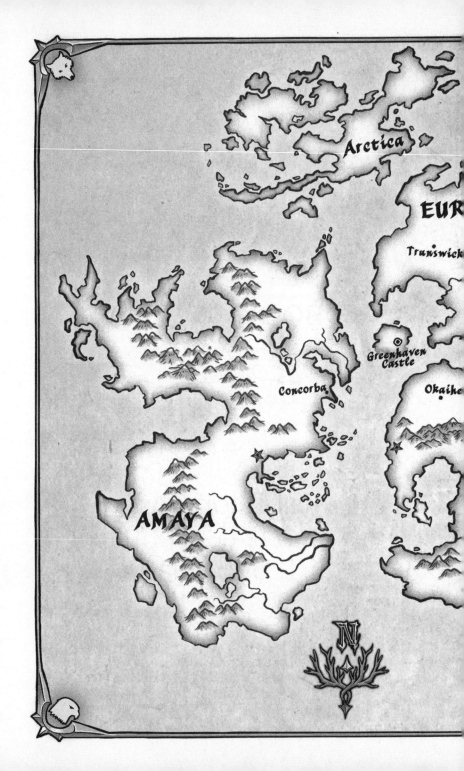

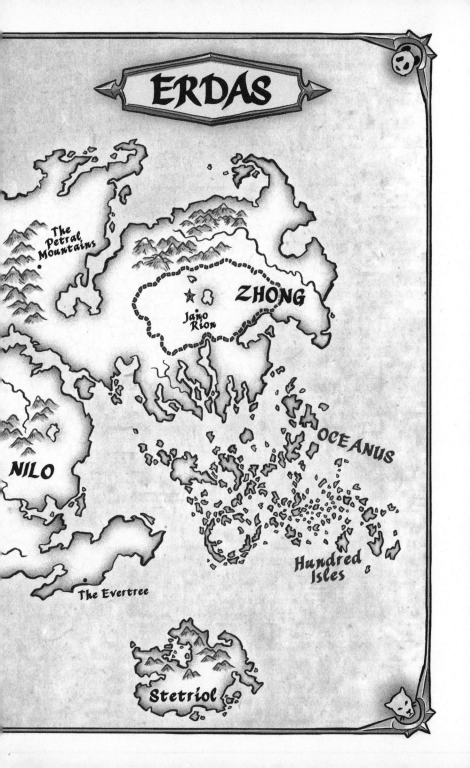

*For Amma, who always took the time to read
comic books with me*
—N.E.

Library of Congress Control Number: 2015944990

ISBN 978-0-545-91098-9

10 9 8 7 6 5 4 3 2 1   15 16 17 18 19

Snake illustration by Angelo Rinaldi. Book frame and lock © LiliGraphie/
Shutterstock. Snake geometric © mw2st/Shutterstock. Leather texture by
CG Textures. Back cover design by SJI Associates and Charice Silverman.

First edition, November 2015

Printed in the U.S.A.   23

Scholastic US: 557 Broadway • New York, NY 10012
Scholastic Canada: 604 King Street West • Toronto, ON M5V 1E1
Scholastic New Zealand Limited: Private Bag 94407 • Greenmount, Manukau 2141
Scholastic UK Ltd.: Euston House • 24 Eversholt Street • London NW1 1DB

WHO IS SHANE?

An introduction by Tui T. Sutherland

*I*T *ISN'T VERY OFTEN THAT A GORILLA AND AN OCTOPUS HAVE a polite conversation.*

It's trickier still when that gorilla is trapped in a cage made of ancient antlers on an enormous rock in the middle of a sunbaked desert, while the octopus lives in the depths of the unknowable ocean.

But Kovo and Mulop are two of the Great Beasts of Erdas, after all, so set aside your questions and imagine the scene . . .

The colossal gorilla hulked his shoulders, baring furious teeth at the prison around him. The sun beat down mercilessly, adding weight to his shaggy black fur until it felt as oppressive as the antlers themselves. Overhead an eagle screamed in the molten air, but Halawir's pity was essentially useless to Kovo.

And then he felt a touch, like a soft tentacle brushing against his brain.

"Get out," Kovo growled.

"Hello, hello," said a deep voice, like bubbles drifting slowly toward the surface. "It has been a long time, has it not? Yes. A long time for a dark soul to be imprisoned, making sinister plans. But it will not be long enough, I think. No, it will not be forever, although it should be."

Kovo snorted, almost chuckling. "Is that what you foresee, you bloviating blob? My escape from here? My glorious triumph over all of Erdas? Because that's what I see in my dreams every night. I don't need mystical foresight to promise you *that's* what's coming."

The octopus made a small humming sound. "Something along those lines. It is a strange and terrible time ahead, I do see that, and so do I, yes. But tell me about this boy king I see at the center of all these plans."

"Aha, yes," Kovo snarled, grinning. "The boy king of Stetriol. A villain through and through. The perfect choice to destroy the world and hand it over to me."

"Hmm," said Mulop again. "Is that so? Such a puzzle. A villain all the way through, you think? I did not know such humans existed. No, indeed, I thought there were measures of good and bad in each of them."

"Ha!" The gorilla turned in an awkward circle, scraping his hide against the points of the antlers. "I know this boy, Shane. He is a traitor and a liar. He burns with vengeance and a thirst for power. He is the perfect puppet for me and Gerathon, and no one will care when we finally crush him and toss him aside."

"I think some will care," murmured Mulop. "He is a brother who loves and fears his sister. He is a friend to a brave Greencloak who cares about him."

"Because she's a fool," Kovo cut in. "She doesn't know the real Shane."

"And you do?" The tentacles fluttered around the corners of Kovo's mind again, light and slithering. "I see a young prince who mourns his family. I see a king who wants to save his people. I see a boy who will regret his mistakes . . . and who will miss his only true friend."

"I see the Devourer." Kovo's eyes glittered with ambition. "Striding to glory beside his fearsome giant crocodile, leading an army of Conquerors to destroy the world. A pawn who will get me everything I want, but who will always be a creature of the Bile. Someone we can control whenever we need to."

"How does someone become such a threat?" the octopus asked. "I have wondered and wondered such a thing. Here's another thing to wonder around and through: When the war is over, what happens to the most hated person in Erdas?"

"Who cares?" The gorilla's laugh rolled across the barren landscape like thunder, sending geckos scrambling into their holes in terror. "When the war is over, I'll be done with him."

"But what happens to villains when they fail?" Mulop's voice seemed to be oozing into the cracks in Kovo's brain. "You're one example, I suppose. Imprisoned and furious for the rest of eternity."

"This eternity is going to be shorter than anyone expects," Kovo snarled.

"What becomes of a king who has lost his army and his country? What becomes of a boy who has betrayed his only friend – and knows it? These are among the few things I do not know, although I think and think upon them."

"You don't need to know." Kovo's meaty hands slammed into the walls of his cage, cutting sharp lines of blood across his palms. "We're not going to fail. Shane will either continue to be our puppet, or if he is too much trouble, we'll kill him."

"We'll see, and so shall we," said Mulop, in his vague, irritating way. "It will be a fascinating story. Can the Devourer ever be forgiven? Is there still a soul in there with any hope of redemption?"

"No," growled Kovo. "Villains are what they are."

"Nobody is the villain of their own story," Mulop said reprovingly. "One thing I know is that even *you* don't see yourself that way."

"True." The gorilla chuckled again, low and sinister. "I have my reasons for the choices I make. But I am the future ruler of all Erdas. This boy king is nobody."

"I am quite certain," said Mulop, "that he would disagree."

"I am quite certain," said Kovo, "that I don't care."

"Someone might care," said Mulop. "If someone were listening with an open mind, and someone could see how complicated Shane's story is, perhaps they would see much more of this Shane than anyone has before."

"Perhaps," said the enormous gorilla with a snort. "If anybody cared enough to tell the story of the boy king of Stetriol. It won't be me." He burrowed his head back on his neck, pulling his shoulders forward as if trying to block out the persistent, blooping voice of the giant octopus.

"Someone must care to tell it," said Mulop thoughtfully, perfectly happy to have this conversation with himself instead. "And someone must care to hear it. Perhaps then, if they know everything he was and will be, they can decide for themselves who Shane really is.

"Traitor, liar, Devourer?

"Failure, puppet, defeated fool?

"Or a boy who thought he was the hero of his own story—who makes terrible mistakes, and has to find a way to move forward when everything goes wrong for him?

"I think the stories will be told, and I think the readers will decide.

"In the end, who is Shane, after all?"

PART 1
VENOM

*Abeke looked to Shane
again. "How awful! Your
bonding . . ."
"Occurred without any
Nectar," Shane said. "I was
one of the lucky ones. Other
friends and family weren't."*

*— Spirit Animals:
Book 1:* Wild Born

SHANE'S LIFE CHANGED FOREVER THE DAY HE WOKE TO the sound of screaming.

It was a scream right out of a nightmare – a sound of terror, and mourning, and fury all tangled together. It was barely human.

He'd never heard anything like it before, yet he knew at once that it was coming from his sister.

Shane leaped from bed and bolted from his room. At some point he stubbed his bare toe on stone, but the pain wouldn't register until much later. At the moment there was only Drina, and the distance that kept him from her. He didn't hesitate, didn't pause at her threshold to wonder what terror awaited him, what monstrous sight could tear such a howl from his sister's throat.

But he paused when he entered the room and its unnatural twilight. His own bedroom had been bright with morning's light, and the hallway too. Something in Drina's room was blocking the light. A frayed and tattered tapestry? Thick strands of cotton? Shane couldn't quite make sense of it.

Drina had stopped screaming, but she lay convulsing in bed. Something was terribly wrong.

He went to her and gripped her by the shoulders, willing her to be still, but her body jumped and jerked beneath his fingers. She looked up at him with eyes that didn't see him. They registered only horror.

He realized he was saying her name, over and over again. "Drina. Drina."

Then he saw movement out of the corner of his eye.

He didn't turn all at once. The hair on the back of his neck stood up, and his ears prickled. He knew somehow that making any sudden moves would be a terrible mistake. So he kept his hands on his sister's shoulders, and turned his head slowly, very slowly, until he was looking into the far corner of the room.

Squatting there in the shadows was the largest spider Shane had ever seen.

It saw him too. It stared back at him with eight eyes, alien and unreadable. Other than the bands of yellow along its abdomen, it was entirely black. Venom dripped from its fangs to the floor.

It stayed absolutely still, and Shane tried to stay still too. But he couldn't suppress a shudder of fear and revulsion.

He had to do something. Others would arrive soon — others must have heard Drina's scream. And the next person through that door would step right beneath those dripping fangs.

He took a heavy brass lantern from Drina's bedside.

He turned away from her slowly, so that he faced the spider. Shane would have to put all his strength behind his throw. He might only have one chance at this.

Those alien eyes stared back, unblinking.

Shane shifted his weight and gritted his teeth. He reared back with the lantern, ready to let it fly when —

Suddenly Drina screamed again. This time, she produced a word: "No!"

She lurched from her bed, shoving into him with all her might. Shane went flying; his head smacked against stone. The world reeled, and he hit stone again, and the lantern shattered all around him, covering him with broken glass.

"He's mine," his sister said. Through a haze of red he watched her take an unsteady step toward the creature on the wall, her arm outstretched, palm up. "He's mine."

It was only then that the true horror of the situation finally dawned on Shane. Despite his fervent hopes, his sister had summoned a spirit animal.

Unconsciousness came for him, and he did not fight it. He didn't want to see what happened next.

Shane never woke slowly. In the two years since Drina had summoned her spirit animal, he jolted awake each morning, usually in a cold sweat, always with a sense of dread. This morning was no different. He immediately scanned the ceiling, then checked the four corners of his bedroom for any sign of an animal. He kept the stone walls bare and the room clear of any clutter: the better to be sure nothing could hide from him. Finally, before daring to place his feet upon the floor, he leaned over the side of his bed, peering into the shadows beneath it like a young child checking for monsters.

It was only after he was satisfied that he had not summoned a spirit animal in his sleep that he remembered to breathe.

Shane knew the odds of being Marked were slim. He reminded himself of that fact every day. Yet despite the odds, every member of his immediate family had summoned an animal. People said they were cursed, and there were times Shane himself believed it.

He was nearly thirteen years old now. If he was going to get a spirit animal – and the bonding sickness that usually came with it – it would happen soon.

Shane slipped from bed and pulled his damp nightclothes over his head. He took a fresh tunic and trousers from his wardrobe – a wooden antique from which he'd removed the doors. That way it was one less hiding place for him to fear. And besides, Shane's uncle had use for any wood he could get his hands on.

As he dressed, Shane remembered a time in his childhood when a servant would wake him, bathe him, dress him. But nearly all the servants were gone now. And it was just as well – there was no money with which to pay them, little food with which to feed them.

Shane knew very little about the lands outside of Stetriol, but he suspected he was the poorest prince in the world.

He walked the long hallway that led to the dining hall, trailing his finger along the stone wall and tapestries, leaving a line in the dust. The tapestries showed legendary scenes of Stetriol's ancient past. On one, torrents of water flowed from the mouth of a frog, creating all the lakes and rivers. Another showed two lizards painting patterns on each other, one with a fine brush and an eye for detail, the other without care.

Shane knew of other tapestries – forgotten tapestries that still hung from the rafters in a dark and disused corner of the castle. Those artworks celebrated other animals entirely: formidable birds of prey, and huge, vicious cats, and an octopus with startlingly intelligent eyes. But the Great Beasts had cursed Stetriol. They were better forgotten.

Lost in thought, Shane jolted with surprise when he rounded a corner and saw a cloaked figure standing before him. He hoped she hadn't seen him flinch, but it was hard to sneak anything past his tutor.

"Yumaris," he said, nodding his head in greeting.

"My prince," she said, lowering her own head in a sort of bow. Shane imagined if she attempted to lower herself any more than that, she might never manage to get up again. She clutched her staff as if without it her heavy robes might drag her to the floor.

He wasn't sure exactly how old she was, but during her history lessons it was easy to imagine that she spoke from personal experience. The oddest thing about her, though, was that she sometimes spoke of the future as if it were history too.

Shane watched curiously as the woman produced a sheathed sword from the folds of her robes. It was the saber he had been training with lately, at his uncle's insistence. "You will be glad to have this blade," she said, holding it out to him.

He wasn't so sure, but he took the sword and affixed it to his belt. "You're my tutor, Yumaris. Aren't you supposed to favor the pen?"

"A prince must have many tools in his arsenal," Yumaris answered, a faraway look in her eyes. "For words and learning do little to impress a jackal."

Shane tightened his belt and gave his tutor a questioning look. "There are no jackals in Stetriol."

Yumaris shrugged. "A figure of speech, my prince. Now, I fear you have more pressing business this morning than breakfast."

Shane sighed. "What is Gar up to this time?"

The throne room was brightly lit, with flaming sconces running along its length. Gar was at the far end, standing on the dais so that he towered over the others assembled around him. He knew better than to actually sit upon the throne, but Shane noticed he stood close enough that he could reach out and touch it.

Gar was Shane's uncle and the king's younger brother. He had no true claim to the throne. But as Shane's nearest living relative who was not confined to bed, Gar had been named regent. In theory, that meant Gar was responsible for advising Shane and teaching him the ways of statecraft. In practice, it meant Gar was more or less in charge until the day Shane was crowned king.

Gar might not have had bonding sickness, but Shane didn't consider him fit to rule. He was hotheaded and cruel. Whereas other members of their family were physically unwell, Gar seemed to have a sickness of the spirit.

"Uncle!" he called out as he crossed the room. "Forgive me for being late. I wasn't aware we were entertaining guests so early."

Gar smiled, but it looked like a grimace. "I see Yumaris found you in time, nephew. Now that you're here, we can begin."

As Shane closed the distance, he took in the scene. There at the foot of the stairs, two guards stood at attention. Between them, a man crouched low, bowing before Gar. The sight made Shane furious.

"And who is this?" he asked, stepping past the guards and ascending the stairs. He only came to a stop once he was a hairbreadth from the throne, closer to it than his uncle was. He loved that throne. It was an ancient masterpiece of iron adorned with a dozen mismatched animal features – wings and scales and antlers – and entirely gray except for the colorful snakes running along its sides. They were red and orange, green and yellow, and rumor had it that King Feliandor himself had added them during his reign, sometime after he had taken to calling himself the Reptile King.

Gar took an awkward sideways step to make room for Shane, and had to turn to address him. "Dear nephew," he began, "this man is a criminal. He stands accused of flouting Royal Edict Thirteen, the rule against –"

"The rule that states all wood in Stetriol belongs to the royal family, for the purpose of rebuilding Stetriol's fleet," Shane finished coldly. "I'm well aware of the edict."

The edict, in fact, was Gar's pet project. He pursued it like a rabid dog. Shane didn't particularly care what the commoners did with their wood, and he knew for a fact that his father didn't care either.

But wood in Stetriol had always been scarce, owing to the mostly arid climate. That was only made worse after the great war and the Greencloak invasion, when the island nation's shores were overrun. After King Feliandor was assassinated and his Conquerors were defeated, the invaders hadn't been content simply to sink Stetriol's entire armada. They set fire to her coastal forests, as well. To this day, wood was exceedingly hard to come by.

People made do. They crafted their homes from stone and clay and iron, all of which were abundant.

But you couldn't rebuild a fleet of ships with stone and metal. And lately Gar seemed very keen to build ships.

"This man," Gar continued, "took an ax to a tree in broad daylight. Given the king's passionate and absolute belief in the necessity of Royal Edict Thirteen, and the boldness of the crime, it is clear he must be swiftly punished."

"You want to make an example of him," Shane clarified.

"As you say, my prince."

"And what does the prisoner say?"

The man at the foot of the stairs did not lift his head. "Your grace," he began. His voice was deep and confident, with an unusual inflection. "I am but a humble commoner and family man. The nights grow cold, and soon snow will fall upon the highlands. I only sought to keep my children warm, to stave off the cold and the illness it brings."

"And so you steal from the crown," said Gar.

"Perhaps if I could make my apologies to the king," he said. "If I could speak to him, one father to another."

Something about that request bothered Shane. He had a sudden suspicion that the man before him knew more than he let on about the condition of Stetriol's king.

"The king—" began Shane.

"The king does not deign to speak to common criminals," Gar spat. "He is a busy man who has made his wishes on these matters known. Guards! Take this 'humble father' to a cell."

The guards lifted the man by his armpits. Shane saw his face for the first time then. He was sunburned, his nose peeling, and his dark beard was unkempt. For all that, though, there was something noble in his demeanor. And his eyes showed no trace of fear.

Most curious of all, though – the man's features and skin tone gave him the look of a foreigner. But Shane knew that was impossible.

"What's your name, stranger?" he asked, almost on impulse.

"Zerif," the man said, and then he was dragged away.

Shane visited Drina every day, but it never got any easier. Sometimes he would walk up and down the hallway for hours, eyeing her bedroom door with dread. A closed door meant Drina was alone with her spider, Iskos, and Shane had no desire to step into their parlor.

An open door, though, meant that Magda was there. Fearless Magda, who each day entered that darkened room, threw wide the shutters, and swept away any cobwebs she could reach. Shane had actually seen her shoo away the monstrous spider one afternoon, as if it were nothing more than a pesky dog underfoot.

Magda was there now, piling dishes upon a tray, and she curtsied when she saw Shane enter. "My prince," she said in greeting.

"Hi, Magda. How is she?"

Magda smiled a small smile. "She's just eaten. You should visit with her while I run to the kitchen and back."

Shane nodded, scanning the room as he slipped into the cushioned chair beside Drina's bed. There were webs in the far corners of the ceiling, but the spider was nowhere to be seen. By this time it was most likely out looking for its own breakfast. Spiders were hunters, and Iskos did not accept any food it hadn't caught itself. Shane shuddered, but was grateful that it sought its meals outside, on the castle grounds.

He took Drina's hand. "Hey," he said.

She turned to look at him, and she smiled from her pillow. They had the same light blond hair, but where his skin was a healthy tan, Drina was so pale as to be nearly translucent. He could see blue veins against her skin, and her hand was cool to the touch.

"No fever today?" he asked, and he smiled back at her. Her eyes were blue and clear and sharp with awareness.

"I feel good," Drina said. "Magda said I may be able to go for a walk this afternoon."

"It's a beautiful day," Shane said.

"I haven't been to the gardens in ages," Drina said. Then she saw Shane's reaction. "What?" she asked.

"Gar is . . . using the gardens right now."

"Ah, he must have taken a prisoner."

Shane nodded. "I hate it," he said softly. "Every time he locks someone away there, I feel like he's tarnishing some part of our childhood."

Drina laughed. Shane hadn't expected that, and he smiled. But the smile died on his lips as Drina's laughter went on. It was a wild sound, aggressive and ugly, and it ended in a harsh cough.

Shane stood, but he froze in place, unsure whether he should go or stay.

"You're *still* a child, Shane," she said once her coughing

had subsided. She threw her blanket aside and placed her bare feet upon the floor. "Gar's never going to respect you. Why should he? Why should anyone?"

Suddenly she pounced, quick as a spider. Before Shane knew what had happened, she had shoved him back, drawn the sword at his hip, and now held him against the wall. She had her forearm against his throat and the blade against his cheek.

He tried to say her name but found he couldn't produce any sound. He felt a drop of hot blood trickling down from where the saber touched him, like a burning tear.

"You're twelve, brother. Just a baby. But you'll be all grown up soon. I wonder what animal you'll get?" Her breath was sour, and her eyes were crazed. "A worm? A slug? Something small and worthless." She pulled away from him, and he slid to the ground, gasping for air.

"It's not fair," she said, dropping the sword so that it clattered on the stone. Just like that, she sounded small and weak again. It seemed to take a great effort for her to pull herself back into bed. "I'd be great. I'd be so great."

As Drina was overtaken by another coughing fit, Shane's hand found the hilt of his saber. He gripped it and watched his sister's convulsing body from her bedroom floor. He reminded himself that she was sick; he told himself it wasn't her fault. But in that moment, he felt no pity for her, and no love – only hate.

Then he saw the handkerchief she held against her mouth. It was wet and heavy with blood.

One of Shane's earliest memories was of panic and pain.

Worse. It was a memory of golden sunlight and happiness that had turned to horror in an instant.

He had been running through tall grass and laughing, chasing a bright white rabbit. The rabbit would wait for him to get close, then hop away, leaving Shane's little arms to close on empty air. Something about the chase struck him, in his wide-eyed youth, as hilarious. He cackled with laughter each time the animal leaped beyond his reach.

Then suddenly there was a snake. In the time it took Shane to blink, the snake darted forward, sunk its fangs into his calf, and retreated back into the grass.

The shock and terror struck first, so that by the time the pain came he was already wailing, rolling around with his face in the dirt.

Drina reached him immediately. He saw fear in her eyes, saw how she hesitated, unsure what to do. It made him cry harder.

But then their mother was there. In his memory, her hands were everywhere at once: cupping the top of his head, wiping tears and snot from his face, ripping away the sleeve of her dress to make a tourniquet. He had no memory of what words she spoke, but to this day he remembered her tone. Her calmness calmed him.

She tied the strip of cloth tightly around his thigh to keep the venom from spreading. And then she lifted him in her arms and carried him back to the castle.

His tears had dried by the time she delivered him to his bed, so he was surprised to realize that Drina was crying now, burying her face in their mother's side.

"Why's Drina crying?" he asked.

"Because she's your sister," their mother answered. "And she loves you. Look here, Drina." She took Drina's chin and turned her tear-streaked face toward Shane. "Your brother is just fine. See?" With her other hand she reached out and ruffled his hair, as light blond as her own. "This is the prince of Stetriol," she said. "He'll never bow to a mere snake."

⸻⟡⸻

The gardens had seen better days, but they were still beautiful. It had been a project of Shane's mother's. She loved the idea of taming a space grown wild, of imposing some small amount of order on the chaos of nature. On the days she was feeling well, she would even get down into the dirt and do the work with her own hands – pulling weeds, planting bulbs. And on the days she wasn't feeling well, she'd usually insist the guards lift her from her bed and carry her there. If she had to spend the day lying down, she said, she may as well have a view.

In her absence, the site had become as overgrown as ever. It was wilder now, but no less lovely for its wildness.

The space had once been home to the royal menagerie, a collection of caged animals. Kings and queens of the past – Shane's ancestors – had kept a variety of creatures here, many of them exotic, captured in foreign lands back before travel to and from Stetriol was banned. But the cages had been emptied out in the early days of the war, when the Reptile King's soldiers had bonded with any animal they could get their hands on.

It boggled the mind. Shane couldn't imagine willingly bonding with an animal. But that was a different time – a time before the bonding sickness.

Many of the cages still stood. His mother had disguised them as best she could with creeping vines and well-placed shrubs. But with the old dungeons long flooded, the king had insisted she leave the cages intact. Just in case.

And now, not for the first time since Gar had become regent, the gardens held a prisoner.

He'd expected to find Zerif pacing his cell or pulling defiantly at the bars. But the man simply reclined against the far wall, seemingly unbothered and lost in thought. He watched as Shane approached. This time, he did not bow.

"The life of a royal," Shane said. "It's so tedious."

Zerif watched him without moving.

"Most people don't realize that," Shane continued. "They assume it's nothing but feasts and dances and horseback riding. But there's a lot of work involved in running a kingdom. Taxes, for instance." Shane waved a stack of parchment paper in the air as he walked up and down alongside the iron bars. "Without taxes, the king is broke. We take it very seriously. We keep records – we write down who pays what, who owes what, going back to when their father's mother's father was granted the little patch of dirt their family still harvests to this day. And in all these many records" – Shane let the stack of papers fall to the ground – "no Zerif. Not a single mention of anyone by that name. How could that be?"

Zerif blinked once, twice, then smiled an oily smile. "I suppose I never got my little patch of dirt."

Shane crossed his arms. "And those poor, freezing children of yours? You don't seem terribly anxious to get back to them."

Zerif shrugged. "So I lied. It is notoriously difficult to get an audience with the king of Stetriol. I gambled that violating his edict would get his attention."

"And what would you do with the king's attention once you had it?"

Zerif rose to his feet. "I have a message for him. Information. I have traveled far and seen much, and I would tell him of the secrets I've learned."

"Tell *me*," Shane said. "I have the authority to act in my father's absence, and—"

"You?" said Zerif. "Or should I speak perhaps to Gar instead? It is confusing to me, who exactly is in—"

"*I am in charge!*" Shane shouted. "Gar is only regent."

"The king is dead," said Zerif. "Isn't he?"

"He is not dead," said Shane. "But he will die before he wastes time on the likes of you." And with that, Shane turned to walk away, content to have the last word.

Or he would have been. But then Zerif said: "Tell him I know the cure."

"What cure?" Shane said without thinking, but when he heard his words he realized he already knew the answer. There was only one cure that mattered—the cure for bonding sickness. In the silence that stretched out then, as Zerif stood there with a smug expression on his face, Shane felt an ache in his stomach. His mouth went dry. He fought to keep the fury in his eyes, as if Zerif didn't have him exactly where he wanted him. As if a cure meant nothing to Shane.

"Tell me," he said at last, his voice breaking on the command.

Zerif sat down again, leaning against the far wall of the cage. "I will speak only to the king."

Shane clenched his fists and his teeth, his whole body becoming a hard knot of muscle and bone. He could feel his heartbeat raging in the small cut on his cheek. "We'll see how you feel after a day with no food." And he stormed out of the gardens, tattered tax documents swirling in his wake.

Shane dreamed he'd summoned an ostrich.

It didn't appear in a burst of light. Instead it grew slowly from his own body. First there was just the tip of its beak, a tough spot on Shane's skin, like a fingernail, where his neck met his shoulder. Slowly the beak grew outward, and then there were eyes, and the feathered head, and the animal's neck, long and sinuous like a snake.

Something went wrong then. The ostrich stopped growing; it was stuck. It was just a head and a neck straining against Shane, desperate to be free from him, screeching and pecking at him and anyone who came close. People kept their distance. But for Shane there was no escape from the ostrich, because the ostrich was him.

Formal occasions were always awkward for Shane. He didn't enjoy being on display, and it was particularly embarrassing in the prince's traditional costume. The outfit was mostly purple velvet, with puffy shoulders, frills at the wrist, and a long, trailing cape. He felt like one of his sister's old dolls.

Still, he smiled big and waved small and tried not to shoot dirty looks at Gar. As regent, his uncle wasn't required to wear any costume at all. Yet the man had chosen to wear the heavy steel breastplate of Stetriol's army.

Stetriol had not had an army in hundreds of years. The breastplate was obviously just for show, brand-new and shining in the sunlight. Shane knew his uncle looked far more impressive than he.

They'd traveled on horseback from the castle and now made their way through the throngs of commoners gathered at the docks. It was not a proper parade, but surrounded by mounted guardsmen, Shane and Gar quickly became the center of attention. The people stepped aside and cheered as they passed, and Shane held his hand aloft and waved as his mother had taught him.

"This isn't a pageant, boy," Gar said under his breath. "What are you doing?"

Shane kept waving and kept smiling. "I'm acknowledging my people. They appreciate it when their leaders smile."

Gar grunted. "In times of peace, maybe."

"We *are* at peace," Shane said. "We're the most peaceful nation in Erdas. The rest of the world pretends we don't exist."

Gar gave no response.

The ship, of course, was impossible to miss. Shane had only ever seen such vessels in drawings, and they somehow didn't do justice to the sight of the thing in life. It was far larger than he'd imagined, five times the size of any dwelling he'd passed on the way here, and made entirely of wood. Its vast sails billowed dramatically, blocking out a huge swath of the sky.

There were several other ships along the waterline, in various states of construction, but there was no question which would be the pride and joy of the fleet. Gar beamed up at it as if he'd built it with his own two hands. He launched himself from his saddle and made his way to the gangplank, leaving Shane to shuffle after him. His velvet suit was not built for speed or agility, and he eyed the plank warily. Finally he had to reel in the heavy purple cape and drape it over his arm, for fear that it might get snagged, or stepped upon, or otherwise manage to trip him up and drag him into the water below.

A tall woman in white leather was there to greet him on deck. She bowed shallowly and said, "My prince."

"This is Admiral Faye," Gar said by way of introduction, and Shane took special notice of the title. A captain was the leader of a ship. An admiral, he knew, was a captain of captains, with command of more than one ship. Stetriol had no captains, let alone admirals. It hadn't had a navy since the great war.

"It's a pleasure," he said.

"King Irwyn sends his regards," said Gar. "He's quite pleased with what you've accomplished here."

The admiral's lips turned up slightly. Her smile was as tight as her steel-gray ponytail. "I am gratified to hear it," she said. "Everything is prepared." She motioned with her fingers, and a man stepped forward to hand her a gleaming silver chalice. She lifted it toward them and then hesitated, seemingly unsure whether to hand it to the prince or the regent.

Gar grunted, stepped forward, and took the cup from her. Red wine sloshed from the rim, dotting the deck like spatters of blood.

"Come on, boy," he said to Shane. "Watch and learn."

It took all of Shane's self-control not to make a face.

Gar and the admiral stepped to the stern, and Shane followed. As soon as they were at the railing, there was a sound of trumpets from below, and the jostling, chattering crowd fell silent and turned their faces upward.

"Good people of Stetriol!" Gar shouted, and his voice echoed in the sudden stillness. "It is my honor as regent to stand before you today to christen this fine ship – the first in Stetriol's new naval fleet!"

A polite cheer rose up, and Gar raised his chalice and waited for the noise to die down. When he could be heard again, he continued: "The war is long over. Long, long over! And yet Stetriol continues to suffer all these years later."

There were a few boos and disapproving whistles from the crowd.

"On this very site, many years ago, we were invaded. Foreigners in green cloaks came to our shores, un-invited and unwelcome. They set our forests on fire. They salted our fields, so no new trees would grow. They put our people in chains, and they murdered our great king."

Shane felt a chill as Gar paused and the silence stretched out.

"The four other kingdoms of Erdas came here together," Gar continued, "to our land, and they told us: 'You, Stetriol, you may not have an army. You, Stetriol, you shall not rebuild your great ships. You shall never leave these shores, and none shall ever visit them.' And for generations, we listened. Now I say, no more!"

The crowd began to cheer again, but there was a wholly different tenor to it now. The noise was louder, coarser, and it went on for much longer. This time Gar did not wait for the noise to subside; he raised his voice and shouted over it.

"We have been ignored for long enough!" he said. "It is time we do as we please within our own borders. And it is time the rest of the world takes notice. Stetriol will not be ignored!"

The layers of velvet wrapped around Shane felt heavy and hot. The sun beat down from above him. The fury in the faces of his people radiated up from below, giving off a heat of their own.

"This ship!" Gar cried out, and Shane wondered how anyone below could hear him now, how anyone was capable of listening. "This ship will henceforth be known as *Prince's Honor*!" He took a sip from the chalice, then splashed the remaining wine onto the deck, making the name official. "For it is our king's will that your own prince, Shane, will command this vessel. And with it, he will sail to the island of the Greencloaks and ensure we are never ignored again!"

Trumpets blared and feet stamped. The crowd chanted their names: "Gar! Gar! Gar!" and "Shane! Shane! Shane!"

Shane looked up at his uncle, who grinned madly back at him, then he turned to regard the crimson-colored wine spattered all across the deck. *His* deck. He knew in that moment that Stetriol would be going to war again. It was inevitable. And he felt certain it would be the death of him.

The first time he'd gone to war, Shane had been eight years old.

It had started quietly. Privately. There had been no great speeches. Instead it came to him like a revelation: It was up to him to wipe out all the snakes of Stetriol.

Thanks to his mother's quick thinking, the venomous bite he'd suffered in the field hadn't been too serious. Still, he was bedridden for several days while his body worked through the toxins. Fevered and nauseous, his dreams were full of sharp fangs and eerie slithering scales. His sister dozed in the chair beside him while Shane felt his pulse in his leg, hammering at the twin puncture marks and the cut the healer had made to bleed out the worst of the venom. And he wondered: *What is the point of a snake?*

He found he could not answer that question. They were worthless and cruel, and he would be the end of them.

Days later, when he was well enough to be on his own, he didn't return to his toys or his wooden fort or his rambles about the castle. Instead he went to the gardener for a shovel. And he went to the tinker for scraps of metal, which he fastened around his shins and calves and forearms. No snake would be able to bite through. He was armed for war.

Shane prowled the castle grounds over the course of a long afternoon, moving slowly and carefully through the grass. He never found a single snake. But as dusk fell, his mother found him.

"Oh, my dear prince," she said, and he turned to see her approaching. "What have you been doing out here?"

Shane shrugged, suddenly worried that he may have done something wrong.

"He wants to hurt the snakes," Drina said, peering out from behind their mother's dress. "Because they hurt him."

It wasn't tattling, exactly. Shane hadn't meant for his war to be a secret one. So why did he feel like he'd been caught?

His mother knelt down to his eye level, but he kept his eyes on the ground. "Most snakes are harmless, Shane. And the one that bit you was only surprised. You don't want to hurt snakes for being snakes, do you?"

Shane shrugged again. "Maybe," he said.

"One day, my love, you will be king. And if you're to be king, you must know mercy."

"But I hate them," he said.

"Oh, I don't think you hate them," said the queen. "I think maybe you're afraid of them."

"I am not!" Shane yelled. "I'm not afraid. They're stupid and I hate them."

His mother tilted her head. "Well. Sometimes hate and fear are the same thing." She unstrapped the piece of tin at each of his forearms, letting them fall to the ground. "Sometimes they go together, walking hand in hand." She removed the guards from his legs. "If you want to prove you're not afraid, then learn to walk among snakes in peace." She winked at him. "But it's always wise to watch your step."

Shane waited anxiously for Magda to leave the room. She was going on and on about some ridiculous story the kitchen staff was spreading about a wild dog stealing meat from the kitchens. "An entire ham!" she exclaimed, and Shane widened his eyes as if he cared.

Finally she took Drina's tray away and Shane slipped into the chair. He kept one hand on the hilt of his sword, just in case, and with his other he shook his sister lightly. He hated to wake her, and he had promised Magda he wouldn't. But this was important. It couldn't wait.

She came to consciousness slowly, blinking at him as if unsure he was really there. "Shane?" she said. "What is it?"

"If I had to leave . . . would you come with me, Drina?"

"What?" she said, looking even groggier than before. "Shane, what are you talking about? Where could we possibly go?"

"Away," he said. "Just . . . away."

He took a moment to steel himself before ascending the tower. It wasn't a steep climb, and the many windows along the spiral staircase meant there were no menacing shadows to contend with. All the same, he was not eager to return to the room at the top of the stairs.

He climbed the stairs anyway.

When they were younger, Shane and Drina had been inseparable. They'd also been natural-born troublemakers, treating the entire castle as their fairground and the harried castle staff as captive playmates. But their father was a stern and serious man — a stern and serious king — and there were days when the safest place to be was out of his way.

So their mother had built them a fort. It was a miniature castle all their own, made entirely of wood. Shane hadn't appreciated at the time just how precious that made it. Surely it was the only one of its kind in Stetriol.

The planks that made up the fort had been painted pink and green — Drina's and Shane's respective favorite colors. The result was garish to Shane's eyes as he looked upon it for the first time in years, but it had seemed perfect back then. There had been just enough space inside for the two of them. Now Shane marveled at how small it was. He hadn't been aware just how much he'd grown in the two years since his sister's panicked screams had signaled the end of their childhood.

He trailed his hand along a pink plank, curled his fingers into the gap, and with sudden violence ripped the board free.

To accept Gar's gift would be madness. It was obvious that his uncle intended to send him into danger, far from the castle. If Shane refused to sail with the fleet, he would look like a coward. If he sailed and somehow managed to survive, by the time he returned, Gar would have solidified his power and crowned himself king.

No, Shane could not accept Gar's gift of a ship. But maybe he could build his own boat. A boat big enough for two. If the old maps of Erdas were correct, Nilo was not so very far away.

Perhaps they'd even have a cure for Drina. Perhaps that was Zerif's secret.

He worked quickly, heedless of the splinters digging their way into his palms, or the blood trickling in around the edges of his ruined fingernails. At some point he realized that he was screaming with each tug. He must have been screaming for some time, though he couldn't remember deciding to do so. But it felt good, so he kept screaming. He screamed each time he pulled a board free, screamed each time he tossed it onto the growing pile behind him.

Eventually he stopped, panting for breath. Sweat streamed down his body, and he felt a salty sting in his hands.

He'd have to get used to labor. But he was better off as a pauper in Nilo than the prince of a sinking ship.

"I think you're a liar," Shane told the man in the gardens' overgrown prison cell.

Zerif lifted an eyebrow but said nothing. He did not stir from his place on the stone floor.

"I *know* you're a liar," Shane corrected. "You already admitted you lied before, to get an audience with my father. So why should I believe you know anything about a cure?"

He worked to keep his voice flat and uninterested. His hands still ached from his efforts in the tower, and he squeezed them together, hoping the pain would make him look distracted.

Zerif shrugged. "As do most men, I tell lies when they might help me get what I want. I am not in the habit of lying for the sake of lying. What would I have to gain from lying about the bonding sickness?"

Shane scoffed. "You must be joking. Do you know how many charlatans we've seen here? Twice a year, some man or woman arrives at the castle gates to hawk an elixir they promise will cure the sick." Shane spit on the ground. "Sugar water. Salt water. One maniac tried to convince my father to drink snake venom."

Zerif's eyes twinkled as if he were amused by some private joke.

"You're just another fraud, preying on the hopes and fears of vulnerable people," Shane said. It was only by digging his fingernails into his cut hands that he was able to keep from shouting.

And then he saw the ham bone lying in the cell.

"Where did you get that?" he demanded.

Zerif shrugged.

"I told the guards you were not to be fed."

"Perhaps your uncle told them otherwise," Zerif suggested. "It must be quite confusing for them. So many masters running around the place."

Shane turned on his heel, but before he could walk away Zerif called out: "Little master, I'll give you this information for free."

Shane didn't turn to face him, but he said through clenched teeth, "I'm listening."

"I'm not some alchemist mixing potions, nor some healer with a noble calling to aid the sick. I do not claim to have the means to cure anything."

Shane turned at that. "You said –"

"I said I know what the cure is. To actually obtain it, I need aid. Aid from the king of Stetriol."

"I don't understand," Shane said. "How do you know anything about the cure if you don't have the means to create it?"

"I overheard the secret," Zerif answered. "At Muttering Rock."

Shane narrowed his eyes. "No one goes to Muttering Rock. It's guarded by Halawir the Eagle. And during the day, it's as hot as a cauldron."

"I do not burn easily," Zerif said, and he tapped his nose, indicating the peeling skin. He did have the look of a man who had spent too long in the wastelands. And there was nothing but wastelands for miles around Kovo's fabled prison.

"One can learn all sorts of secrets," he said, "if one takes the time to listen at the base of that great pillar. You might even hear the strangest conversations passing between a warden and his prisoner." He retook his seat. "Tell your father I'm in the mood to share. But only with the king of Stetriol."

Shane dreamed he'd summoned a seal.

He stood upon the beach and watched it play in the surf. From time to time it would clamber onto shore, graceless and awkward as it hobbled across the sand like a dog with its back legs tied together. It looked up at Shane, its dark eyes shining, and grunted once – an invitation.

Then it pulled itself back across the sand and into the water, where it was free and happy and could move again with grace.

But Shane wasn't allowed in the water. He knew he'd never be free.

The castle had become a dark and quiet place in the years since the queen had died, as if the entire structure were her tomb.

Shane's mother had possessed many skills beyond the talents she displayed in the gardens. One of the most impressive was her ability to calm the people around her, to talk them down from their fears and keep them happy. Once she died, more guards and servants left the castle with each passing year. They were nervous about being around so many spirit animals, as if the bonding sickness might be contagious—as if they put their own children at risk by their proximity to the "cursed" descendants of the Reptile King.

For many, Iskos had been the final straw. Spirit animals were one thing, but a spirit animal with eight hairy legs and venomous spit was another thing entirely.

To Shane's mind, the sole advantage to the situation was that much of the castle had been roped off and abandoned. So it was an easy matter for him to steal what he needed. The old lance held by an ornamental suit of armor would serve as a paddle. The extra silverware forgotten in a cupboard could be traded for food. And a tapestry—a tapestry would make a perfect sail.

He strolled along a quiet hallway, the thick layer of dust at his feet muffling his footfalls. He hadn't set his eyes on these artworks since he was a boy, and they were more stunning than he'd remembered. There was Suka, a white bear set against an icy background. And Cabaro, a great cat with a mane of golden hair, baring his teeth from a rocky outcropping above a field of grass. There was the tusked pig, and the white bird with the long, delicate neck—Rumfuss and Ninani. He struggled to remember their names, for the Great Beasts were all but ignored in Stetriol, and most held the forms of animals he'd never actually seen.

But his mother had taught him all of their names. Even the names of the Four Fallen, who had defied Tellun the Elk's vow of noninterference when they'd aided the Greencloak invasion. *Those* four were not represented on the tapestries. If they'd ever been part of the set, they had most likely been burned to ash in the aftermath of the war.

Missing, too, were Gerathon and Kovo, who had sided with Stetriol. The invaders had probably burned those tapestries themselves.

In the end, Shane chose Mulop. The oddness of the octopus appealed to him. It would be an ungainly thing on land, but quite at home in the sea. And the sea was where Shane was heading.

He ripped it free from the wall and hid his face in the crook of his arm while the dust he'd stirred up swirled about him and settled in his hair, on his shoulders. When he lifted his eyes again, his gaze fell upon a portrait farther down the hall. He knew instantly whom it depicted.

Rolling up the tapestry and shoving it under his arm, he drifted over for a better look.

It was a painting of his ancestor, Feliandor. Or "Good King Fel." Or "The Reptile King." Most surviving imagery of the king showed a strapping young man girded for war, usually sitting astride a massive crocodile. But Feliandor had become king at a young age, and here he was in the first year of his reign, a boy no older than Shane.

His chin was up and his shoulders back, but the artist had captured some emotion in the young king's eyes that was not pride or confidence. It looked to Shane like fear. As if it were taking all of the boy's willpower to sit still with the oversized crown balanced upon his head. As if the crown might fall at the very moment he was to be immortalized in brushstrokes.

"You poor fool," Shane said. "You should have gotten out while you could." He looked over the portrait for a moment more, and decided he didn't see much of a resemblance.

"What's in it for you?" Shane asked Zerif on the third night of his imprisonment.

"Come again?" Zerif asked languidly.

"You claim you do not lie for the sake of lying," Shane said. "But I'd wager you're no more likely to tell the truth for its own sake. How do you benefit, traveling all the way here from the dead center of the continent to share a muttered secret with the king?"

Zerif smiled. "Perhaps I'm just a generous soul."

"So smug," Shane said, feeling a little smug himself. "So convinced that your secret gives you power over the powerful."

"Would I be wrong to think so?"

"Not wrong," Shane answered. "Provided your secret stayed secret."

Zerif stood and stretched, seemingly unconcerned. At length he responded, "I suppose you expect me to guess what you've guessed? A clever trick to make me show my hand?"

"Not hardly. I don't need to trick you. I may not know the riddle, but I've guessed the answer: Bile."

Shane watched the man's face closely, so he saw the briefest flash of fury cross his features. An instant later, he appeared as calm as ever, but too late – Shane knew he'd guessed right.

"See, I've been thinking about our Good King Fel – the Devourer, as the rest of the world knew him. I saw his portrait earlier, and I haven't been able to get him out of my head. He was the last king of Stetriol to actually *want* a spirit animal, and legend has it that Kovo made it possible by providing a substance known as Bile. Feliandor's soldiers all used the Bile, and none of them suffered the bonding sickness. That only happened after the war – when the secret to creating the Bile was lost. A secret known to Kovo. Who is imprisoned . . . at Muttering Rock."

Zerif glowered for a moment, but then a smile broke across his face, and this time it seemed genuine. "Not bad," he said. "You've only got the barest understanding of the big picture, but you're not wrong."

"So tell me the rest of it," Shane said. "Or else I go to Muttering Rock myself and cut you out entirely."

"The king is dead. Isn't he?"

"If he is, then I'm the king. Either way, you deal with me."

Zerif sighed. "Kovo wants to help. As does his jailor."

"Halawir the Eagle? Why would –"

"Halawir has long been sympathetic to Stetriol. It pains him to see your people suffer – on that, he and Kovo agree. They say that the Jade Serpent will be your salvation, and it's here, in the capital. Somewhere only the king can get it."

"The Jade Serpent?" Shane asked.

"A talisman," Zerif answered. "Gerathon's talisman, to be specific. According to Kovo, Stetriol's true king has it." He leveled his steely gaze at Shane. "Is that you or not?"

Shane's muscles burned, and now the fire was spreading to his mind. He'd lost track of how long he'd been at work – sawing and sanding and hammering on an abandoned beach, the sound of the surf in his ears. He'd worked through the night and all day long, and now it was night again. His boat was an ugly thing, that was certain – mismatched boards of pink and green, cotton stuffed in every crevice, then slathered with tar, all straight lines so that it looked more like a box than the magnificent ship he'd boarded days before. But the book he'd taken from the royal library indicated that it would float, and that was all that mattered.

He could hardly stay focused on what he was doing. Much of the work was repetitive, and he found his mind wandering again and again to Zerif's words. To the Jade Serpent. Did his father have it?

Did Gar?

Would that mean Gar was the true king of Stetriol?

And why did that gall Shane so deeply, when he only intended to leave?

When the moon clouded over, he decided he had done enough. He pulled his project along the beach and found a thick bramble of shrubs where the sand met an inlet, a little stream running out to the ocean. It was the best hiding spot he could manage, and close enough to the water that he'd be able to make a hasty escape when the time came.

He knew he had to go. But he also knew he couldn't leave, if the cure he'd hoped for all along was here.

Bleary-eyed and sore, he made his way back to the castle, following the stream and the scrubby plants running its length. The waterway grew wider and deeper as he went, and the only sounds in the night were its gentle burble . . . and a rustling noise ahead, like someone stepping carefully through the brush.

The moon broke through the clouds, and Shane could just make out a figure ahead, leaning over the stream as if examining its reflection.

"Drina?" he whispered.

The figure turned, and Shane had to laugh, because it wasn't his sister — wasn't even a person. It was a kangaroo. He'd never seen one so close to the castle grounds before.

Their eyes met, and Shane expected the animal to hop away, but it didn't. It just stood there, considering him, and Shane was struck again by just how human it appeared. There was intelligence in those eyes, as if the kangaroo were puzzling him out.

"There's no need to bow, friend," Shane joked.

And then there was an explosion of water, and a monster leaped from the stream to smash its jaws down around the kangaroo's head.

It happened in an instant, but Shane saw every detail: the teeth piercing the animal's flesh, and the way its neck twisted at an angle that was all wrong as the beast dragged it down into the water. There was panic in the kangaroo's eyes in the moment before they were submerged. Its legs kicked out blindly while the crocodile held its head beneath the surface and thrashed. One kick, two kicks, and then the kangaroo went still.

It was over before Shane could react. He howled in protest, drew his sword, and charged, but too late – the kangaroo was already dead.

All he managed to do was draw the crocodile's attention.

It was a massive beast with soulless eyes glowing like flat, white disks in the moonlight. Its body – what he could see of it above the waterline – appeared carved out of the same stone as his castle, but older, showing more cracks, and dents, and sharp edges. Its teeth glistened black with fresh blood as it opened its mouth to hiss.

And then it pulled itself onto shore, heading straight for him.

Shane waved his sword in the croc's direction and

screamed, hoping to deter it, but it showed no sign of being impressed. He changed tactics, turning to run with only yards between them – and he slipped.

Shane fell, sprawling into the dirt. But he kept his grip on the saber. Lifting himself up on one hand, he twisted to face the predator as it bore down on him. He could see straight down its fleshy gullet.

Then, from out of nowhere, a wild dog bounded onto the croc's back, snapping and snarling.

It was all the distraction Shane needed. He scrambled to his feet and ran, only daring to look back once he was clear of the brush and halfway across an empty field. The animals had not given chase.

Only then did Shane realize what an odd sight it had been. A wild dog attacking a crocodile? He'd never heard of such a thing. And if he didn't know better, he'd have sworn the dog was no dingo. It was a smaller, lither animal. It looked like images of jackals he'd seen in books.

But there were no jackals in Stetriol.

Despite his exhaustion, Shane did not go straight to bed. He went instead to the gardens. The guards stationed at its entrance startled at the sight of him.

"My prince," they said, one after the other. And then the boldest asked, "Uh, what brings you here at this hour?"

"The hour is irrelevant," Shane answered. "It's well past time the prisoner had an audience with my father."

Shane had rarely been to his father's quarters. He'd always feared the man.

King Irwyn did not abide weakness. He refused to acknowledge that he suffered from bonding sickness, even as that sickness took its toll, wearing away at him over the years. He refused, too, to admit that his wife had been sick. But when his daughter—his firstborn—was similarly stricken, something in the king had snapped.

"Behold the king of Stetriol," Shane said. "My fearsome father."

Zerif, for the first time, seemed at a loss for words.

The king's eyes were open, but vacant. A thin line of drool hung suspended from his slack lips.

"Is he . . . still in there?" asked Zerif. His hands were shackled, and Shane felt certain the man posed no threat. He had dismissed the guards and his father's caretaker, so that they could speak in private. He honestly didn't know whether Irwyn could hear them or not.

"We don't know," said Shane. "Gar claims to speak with him, but he's lying. He says that so people will do what he wants. To contradict him, I'd have to publicly admit that the king is . . . unfit. That Stetriol is without a true leader." Shane sighed. "His last act was to name Gar regent, to act in his stead until I become king. So as long as my father lives, I can't take the throne—can't even touch it, according to our laws, and Gar continues to have . . . influence."

" 'So long as he lives.' Do you call this living?"

Shane shrugged sadly. "It isn't death, exactly."

"I've never known bonding sickness to ruin a mind so completely."

"It wasn't bonding sickness that did it."

"No?"

Shane tugged at his own hair tiredly. "Don't get me wrong—he was sick, all right. But the real trouble happened when he decided he could cure himself. He decided . . . He thought . . . Well, he killed it. He killed his own spirit animal."

Zerif sucked breath through his teeth. "That would be like killing a piece of yourself. Like cutting off your own limb."

"Some animals will gnaw off their own limbs to escape a deadly trap." Shane frowned. The room smelled sour, and he felt his sleepiness bearing down on him. "I don't know. Maybe we're cursed after all."

"Maybe you are," Zerif said. "But it's not the fault of any Great Beast. It's the Greencloaks who have done this to you." He rotated his hands in their manacles, rattling his chains. "That's the other piece of news I intended to give the king. And here's my audience, I suppose."

"Go on," Shane said, his sleepiness receding.

There was a flash of light, and suddenly a jackal stood beside Zerif, watching Shane with curious eyes that reminded him very much of Zerif's own.

"Just as I suspected," Shane said. "You have a spirit animal."

"Yes."

"You don't seem sick."

"No."

"You've been cured?"

Zerif shook his head. "I was never sick. Here's the truth, Prince Shane: The Greencloaks cured the bonding sickness long, long ago. Everywhere but here—and here, whether by curse or foul luck, the sickness is more common than it ever was anywhere else in Erdas. Despite this, the Greencloaks have ignored your plight." He ran a shackled hand along his beard. "They left your people to suffer while they silently took over the rest of the world."

Shane ground his teeth together and growled like a cornered animal. "Tell. Me. Everything," he commanded.

The Jade Serpent had been right under Shane's nose all along.

He realized it as soon as he had Zerif repeat Kovo's words. "Tell me exactly what he said," Shane insisted.

"'The Jade Serpent is where only Stetriol's king may retrieve it, hidden away in his seat of power.'"

Zerif had assumed the king's "seat of power" was the capital, or the keep. He wasn't thinking literally enough.

"The throne," Shane guessed. And sure enough, when he touched the throne for the first time, tugging at the ornamental snakes, one of them came free in his hand. A heavy green snake carved from jade.

The sense of triumph he experienced in that moment was nothing compared to what he felt when, at Zerif's bidding, he submerged the talisman in a bowl of murky swamp water. The water changed instantly, becoming a warm amber color, almost glowing with its own light. Shane didn't doubt for an instant that it was magic.

Drina grimaced as she drank it in the morning, and Shane frowned to see the sour twist in her features, bracing himself for her verbal abuse. But she swallowed, and blinked her eyes rapidly, and then she broke into a smile.

"How do you feel?" he asked her.

And he knew the answer just by looking at her. Her cheeks were a healthy shade of pink. Her fever was gone, and her blue eyes caught the sunlight, flashing a bright, vibrant yellow.

The curse had been broken.

Shane stood upon the beach that night and watched his sad little handmade boat go up in flames.

It was his thirteenth birthday. And no one in his family had ever summoned a spirit animal later than age twelve.

Which meant he was free. The one thing he'd always feared above all others had not come to pass.

He used to ask himself what kind of person would *want* a spirit animal.

Now he regarded the amber fluid in the stoppered vial, holding it up to the dancing light of the flames, and he thought he knew the answer.

Two castle guards came crashing through the dry brush at the edge of the beach. They saw Shane there and they bowed, immediately and deeply, planting their knees into the sand.

"The . . . the king is dead," one of them said. "Long live the king."

"My father is dead?" said Shane flatly. "What happened?"

The guards kept their heads bowed. They seemed hesitant to answer.

"Well?" said Shane.

"A . . . a dog," said one.

"Some kind of wild dog," continued the other. "It got into the castle and tore out his throat. We don't know where it came from."

They kept their eyes turned toward the sand, giving Shane a quiet moment for anger or for grief.

He felt neither. But while their eyes were averted, he allowed himself a furtive smile.

"Sire, if there's anything we can do—"

"There is one thing," said Shane, and he slipped the vial into a pocket over his heart. "I'm going to need a crocodile. A live one. A *big* one. I know just where you should look."

What kind of person would want a spirit animal?

A ruler, thought Shane.

A king.

Shane dreamed he'd bonded with a crocodile.

It was the largest beast he'd ever seen: a prehistoric nightmare with razor-sharp teeth and pitiless eyes. They brought it into his throne room in chains, but it had not come easily. The creature had drowned one man and maimed two others before it had been subdued. All who looked upon it felt awe.

Shane drank down the Bile in one gulp, and the crocodile was his.

He woke slowly from an untroubled sleep. For a moment, he worried it had just been a dream.

Then he looked down at his bare torso, and saw the image of the crocodile branded there.

And Shane knew there would no longer be any question who was in charge.

PART 2
VENDETTA

She saw Halawir give one mighty thrust and then furl his wings, shooting up out of the great hall. The Great Beast disappeared into the sky, along with Shane.

– Spirit Animals:
Book 6: Rise and Fall

SHANE CLOSED HIS EYES AND SMILED INTO THE WIND. HE allowed himself to enjoy one perfect moment of total victory.

The war was over, and he'd won it.

For months, he had been seeking fifteen talismans of great power from all across Erdas. Any one of the talismans had the power to change the world.

Shane had eleven of them. Eleven! And three more were in the hands of his army.

He whooped, pumping his fists into the air, then felt his balance lurch dangerously and brought his hands back down to grip Halawir's feathers. He was riding cross-legged on the back of the massive eagle, and every time Halawir flapped his wings, Shane swayed.

Since leaving his home some months ago, Shane had seen many amazing sights. He had climbed the mountains of Amaya, scaled Zhong's great wall, and sailed the seas from the rigging of his very own warship.

But he'd never been anywhere near this high up before.

It was as if all of Erdas were spread out before him. The sea sparkled below like a shifting landscape of precious gemstones, ringed by two great landmasses. At this height he couldn't even tell the difference between Nilo and Eura. They were identical swaths of green spreading out to distant mountains.

But who needed to tell them apart anymore? What was the point of borders, anyway? It all belonged to him now.

He lifted his hands again, slowly this time, and leaned into the wind, grabbing at clouds that puffed away to nothing in his fingers. The cold wind brought tears to his eyes, but he fought to keep them open.

"Pleased with yourself?" said Halawir. As a Great Beast, he was able to communicate without actually opening his imposing curved beak. Shane heard the mighty animal's voice in his head, clear and piercing, and he winced.

"Yes!" he answered, shouting his reply into the wind. "Yes, I'm very pleased. We've won, Halawir. That was it! The Greencloaks are finished."

"I confess, you achieved your objective much faster than any of us expected."

It was the closest thing to a compliment Shane had ever heard from the bird – Halawir was majestic but pompous, and usually gave Shane the impression that he'd rather be anywhere else than in the company of humans. But the two of them had more in common than Halawir might like to admit.

They'd both been lying for a very long time, hiding their true natures, like a crocodile hides beneath the surface of the water, waiting to strike.

In truth, Shane's infiltration of Greenhaven had gone nothing like he'd intended. Abeke's friends had exposed him almost immediately. His original plan had involved a lot more sneaking around, and he'd almost been looking forward to spending some time on the island. The days he'd spent on the boat with Abeke had been . . . Well, they had been a pleasant respite from months of war.

The fact that Shane's true identity had been revealed and

he'd *still* been able to get away with all of the Greencloaks' talismans made his victory all the sweeter.

"Did you see the look on Olvan's face?" he called out to Halawir. "When he realized he'd been beaten? Priceless!"

Halawir opened his mouth and emitted a piercing cry. Shane wondered for a moment if that was his version of laughter – and then the bird veered sharply to the side, nearly throwing Shane off into open air.

"Hold on, mammal!" said Halawir. Rather unhelpfully, Shane thought. There was not much else Shane could do.

Halawir dove, dropping several yards in a single second, and Shane felt as if they had left his stomach in their wake. Before he could complain, he saw a sphere of dull gray metal, larger than a coconut, whiz past, arcing above his head. If Halawir hadn't acted so quickly, it would have smashed right into them. And judging from the speed at which it plummeted back down toward the sea, it was frightfully heavy.

"Was that . . . Was that a cannonball?" Shane shouted.

"We are under attack."

Shane followed the arc of the cannonball back to its origin and saw a ship on the sea below. It was long and narrow – a schooner, built for speed. Its sails were bright green.

"Greencloaks," Shane hissed. So they must have managed to get a ship out from Greenhaven to follow him after all. There was an explosion on the deck of the ship, a cloud of smoke, and Shane shouted, "Incoming!"

He brought his head back around and leaned in low, hugging Halawir's body as the great bird tilted. For one terrifying moment, Shane's feet were in midair, his grip on the slick feathers the only thing keeping him from twisting away in the wind – and then Halawir leveled, and Shane came crashing down.

"Have a care!" Shane shouted. "Lose me and you lose the talismans."

Halawir screeched again. This time there was no mistaking the sound for laughter.

"It's a sailboat!" Shane cried. "Don't you have power over the winds?"

"They have whales pulling the boat," Halawir answered. "And there is only so much I can do with a rodent tugging at my feathers."

Shane ignored the insult. "Then we need to get over land, where whales can't follow," he said.

Halawir made no reply but veered south, toward Nilo.

Shane gritted his teeth. He had a sword sheathed at his hip – useless from up here. He had nearly a dozen talismans of formidable power – but couldn't risk sorting through them when it was all he could do to hold on.

If there was one thing Shane couldn't stand, it was feeling powerless. He'd had enough of that back in Stetriol.

But he hadn't truly been powerless in a long time. Not since he'd drunk the Bile and joined Zerif in his campaign against the Greencloaks.

"Grahv!" he called. "I need you." The tattoo that wrapped across his chest and down his stomach flared with light, and then was gone, and Shane caught just a glimpse of his crocodile's great scaled tail as the animal plunged into the sea below.

"That will slow them down," he said. "Grahv is more than a match for a couple of whales."

"A momentary reprieve," Halawir replied. "We can't allow ourselves to be tracked back to camp."

"Why not? Let them come in force," Shane scoffed. "I took them on single-handedly. What chance would they have against my army?"

"No chance," said Halawir. "But creatures who cannot fly are easily surrounded, and we do not have time for a drawn-out siege. Not when we are so close to freeing Kovo."

Shane nodded. There was no sense drawing out the conflict just because the Greencloaks didn't know when they were beaten. "Then you'll have to lead them away," he said. "I'll make my own way home."

"Across Nilo?"

"I've got Mulop's talisman," Shane replied. "I'll swim."

"Very well," Halawir said. "But do not tarry. You would not wish to displease Gerathon."

"I know that," Shane spat. His face grew warm despite the blustery wind. "I know that well."

Halawir scudded to the coastline, so low that the trees below shook in his wake.

"Now would be an opportune time," he said. "While our pursuers are occupied."

Shane waited until Halawir was gliding, before the next flap of the Great Beast's wings brought an increase in speed. They were still going too fast for his liking. They were still too high.

But Shane was used to doing the best he could with poor options.

He let go of Halawir's feathers and pushed off into the sky.

Shane dreamed of spiders.

He was roaming the corridors of the castle where he'd lived as a boy. Everything was just as he remembered – but there were spiders everywhere.

Big spiders and small spiders. Spiders marked with red diamonds and yellow stripes and brown spots. Hairy spiders and smooth, shiny spiders that appeared wrought from black metal.

They'd taken up residence in the castle Shane had left behind, and as he made his way through the hallways, he was forced to step through one web after another. He swept his arms out ahead of him, slapping the webbing aside, but it clung to him, and he ended up with strands in his mouth and his hair and tickling at his ears. He was sure some of the spiders themselves were on him too. He couldn't spare the time to look, but he could feel them skittering across his skin.

He had to find Magda. When he'd led his forces to war, he'd left his family's kindly servant behind. For her to have let the castle fall into such a state – something was obviously wrong.

The webs slowed his progress but couldn't stop him, and eventually he caught sight of an open door ahead. As he approached, a figure stepped into the doorway from within, blocking his way. It was Magda.

The look on her face was grave. "You may not enter, my prince."

"I'm not a prince," Shane said. "I'm the Reptile King."

He pulled his collar aside to show her the crocodile tattoo, but it was completely obscured by spiderwebs.

Shane looked up at Magda, and he caught a glimpse of something beyond her—a human figure on the bed. A girl . . .

"Who is that?" Shane asked.

"Don't look," Magda said, but without any emotion in her voice. "Don't look."

The shadows in the room shifted, and Shane thought he might get a better look at the figure. But then he realized it wasn't shadows obscuring his view but spiders, a whole sea of spiders, swarming over every surface of the room. Was there even a girl on the bed, or only a thousand spiders in the shape of a girl?

The spiders were on Magda too, Shane realized. How had he not noticed before? They were crawling all over her. Most of them were small, skittering in and out of view. But clinging to her arm was a massive specimen, black and yellow, and it was sinking its fangs into the pale flesh of her arm.

Shane tried to scream for her, but the name on his lips was . . .

"Drina!"

Shane awoke in a sweat, to find his vision filled with green.

He was on his back, staring up into the canopy of a forest.

His back hurt. His head hurt. He had a nasty cut on his forearm, no doubt from plummeting through the trees.

But when he brought his hand to the pocket of his leather tunic and the talismans were still there, he let out a sigh of relief.

He sat up and took them from his pocket for the first time. Each talisman was a pendant in the shape of an animal – a Great Beast – and each bore a portion of the beast's power. There was an eagle wrought in bronze that bore a striking resemblance to Halawir, and a delicately detailed swan carved from marble. The wolf and the lion were made of precious metals, silver and gold, but the most beautiful to Shane's eye was the leopard of amber. It seemed to glow with its own inner light.

Shane was slow to realize there was no octopus. No octopus, and no ram either.

He checked his pocket again, but he knew he wouldn't find them there. He scanned the ground around him, but the talismans had all been one great tangled mass in his tunic. There would have been no way for one or two to slip loose. Which meant . . .

Which meant he'd left two behind. In the hands of the Greencloaks.

Shane leaped to his feet and screamed. He kicked at the dirt and paced in a tight circle, clenching his fists. He wanted to hit something, but there was nothing in reach but the trees.

There was no use going back. Even if he could get to Greenhaven again, it wasn't worth the risk. He had nine talismans, and he'd left Zerif with three. He just had to hope that twelve were enough to breach Kovo's prison. With Kovo released, Shane's obligations to Gerathon would at last be fulfilled. And he, Shane, would rule over a new world order free of the tyranny of the Greencloaks.

Shane took stock of his possessions. He had his sword, a stoppered vial of Bile that had somehow not shattered when he'd fallen from the sky, and the talismans. Nothing else but the clothes on his back and the tattoo that had reappeared on his chest.

He thought grimly that it said something significant about his life that he was lost in the wilderness with Gerathon's Bile in his pocket, but no drinkable water.

He put away all the talismans except one: a falcon made of copper. He gripped it in his hand and found a tall tree with low branches. Shane had grown up a prince in a castle, but he was far from pampered, and the past year had made him strong. He climbed the tree quickly, his movements confident, and in a matter of seconds he broke through the canopy to the infinite expanse of blue beyond it.

Shane slipped the Copper Falcon's cord around his neck, and instantly his eyesight sharpened.

"Wow," he said. So this was what it was like to see the world through Essix's eyes.

He could see a drop of water on a leaf three trees over. He could see a distant dragonfly, its wings buzzing madly as it rose above the trees. And there, far off across the ocean, he could see an eagle—a massive eagle made small by distance, pursued across the ocean by a ship. Their ploy had worked.

He turned in the other direction. The Conquerors' camp was too far even for his keen eyes to see. If he could fly or swim, he'd be there in no time. On foot, it would take him days.

He sighed, climbed down to the forest floor, and started walking.

To avoid getting lost, Shane kept the coastline in view. To avoid being seen, he walked just within the tree line, where the forest gave way to Nilo's beaches. That meant weaving among the trees—there was no natural path. It was slow going, but it was prudent. And Shane had no great desire to plunge deeper into the forest, where the trees grew so thick they blocked out the sky.

Soon the choice was taken from him. The sandy beaches gave way to pebbles, and then to great rocks, and the ground sloped up steeply so that the only way to follow the coastline would be to scale sheer cliffs. He might have managed it with the Granite Ram of Arax . . . but that was one of two talismans still under Greencloak control.

So Shane stepped deeper into the forest.

Here, at least, there was water from the occasional freshwater streams. He had no waterskin, so he was forced to drink as he went, and frequently. The air was muggy beneath the trees, and Shane was soon sweating. Berries grew in clusters wherever water touched the soil, but they were unfamiliar to him and he deemed them not worth the risk. With each passing hour, however, his hunger grew.

To distract himself, he decided to familiarize himself with the talismans, careful to use only one at a time. Used together, the talismans exerted control over something called the Evertree. The three Great Beasts who backed Shane had been guarded in their descriptions of the mysterious tree, but one thing they had made abundantly clear: The Evertree was the key to curing the bonding sickness that had swept over Stetriol like a plague. The tree had suffered some kind of damage in the last great war – this was where bonding sickness had come from – and all fifteen talismans would be needed to heal it. Using a handful of the talismans at once, however, would more likely cause the tree more damage, and Shane wouldn't be responsible for that.

He knew Cabaro's lion was supposed to bestow its wearer with a ferocious roar. He decided not to try it out, for fear of drawing unwanted attention. Same for the Slate Elephant of Dinesh, which would dramatically increase the size of his spirit animal. Even if there were room among the trees for an elephant-sized crocodile, it wouldn't help him blend in.

Jhi's Bamboo Panda made him feel suddenly refreshed. The ache he felt from his fall disappeared the moment he placed the charm around his neck, and didn't return when he removed it again. Halawir's talisman allowed him to nudge the air around him, the way his hand might divert the water in a stream. The Silver Wolf of Briggan sharpened his senses of smell and hearing just as the Copper Falcon had sharpened his eyesight. The effect was almost overwhelming in a forest teeming with unseen life and activity. Kovo's Obsidian Ape likewise enhanced his vision, but in a subtly different way than the falcon did. Shane couldn't quite put his finger on the difference. He examined a tree trunk in the distance, and it came into sharp relief. He could see the lichen growing upon its bark, the stress points where it might be felled with a single well-placed ax blow. Something about the effect was unsettling, and Shane removed the pendant and stuffed it back into his tunic.

In the end, he opted to wear the Amber Leopard of Uraza. It bestowed a feline grace to his movements, allowing him to move more quickly through the trees and avoid the knotted roots that tried to trip him up every dozen yards. It made him feel at ease in this Niloan jungle Uraza had once called home.

. It was simply the most practical choice, he told himself.

Night was falling when Shane at last came upon a village.

The forest was so thick with trees that its daytime was like a green-tinged twilight. Shane thought he'd lose track of day and night entirely, but it wasn't so – the forest was definitely getting darker, and the tenor of animal sounds was shifting as nocturnal frogs and insects overtook the birdsong that had accompanied him throughout his long afternoon hike. He knew it would be wise to stop soon.

When he saw the trees parting ahead and a cluster of huts in the clearing beyond, his heart soared . . . and his stomach grumbled. But his relief was short-lived. The torches at the outskirts of the village were cold; there was no light beyond what the dusk provided, and no human sounds among the chirp and wail of the insects.

Shane stepped into the clearing and knew at once that this village was a carcass – a dead remnant of a thing once living. Half the huts were burned out, their walls black and blistered and their thatched roofs collapsing. The wooden benches ringing the central fire pit had been knocked over and the animal pens hacked apart, fences swung wide.

Everywhere he looked there were signs of violence and panic. The village was not just dead — it had been murdered.

The people, however, seemed to have escaped. There were no bodies among the wreckage.

Shane sighed and wiped the sweat from his brow. Perhaps it was just as well. This way, he didn't have to explain what he, a young noble from Stetriol, was doing wandering the Niloan jungle alone. But he had been looking forward to a meal. His stomach grumbled again, and this time it was echoed in a rumble of thunder overhead. Shane looked up. The village stood in a clearing, so he had a view of the sky for the first time in hours. The fading light of the sun illuminated storm clouds rolling in from the coast.

He walked among the empty huts until he found one that had been left intact. It had no door, just an open doorway, and Shane knew that said much about the people who had lived here. They had trusted their neighbors. That had apparently been a mistake.

He stepped into the doorway as thunder rumbled once more and the wind picked up. Shane could smell the rain coming and was glad for shelter, whatever had become of the people who'd built it.

The space, a single room, was simple. There was a bed of straw against the far wall, and various agricultural tools hanging from hooks. He searched a series of chests and found clothing, a tattered hidebound book, and a child's doll, but nothing to eat. He caught a whiff of something foul, and realized it was his own body—he was soaked through with sweat.

Shane pulled off his boots with some effort, and his toes throbbed with relief. He removed Uraza's talisman and put it and all the others into his left boot, then shoved both boots under the straw bed. He untied his tunic and shrugged out of it, hanging it from an empty hook. Immediately the night breeze from the open doorway cooled his clammy skin, spreading gooseflesh across his chest.

He crawled into the bed, traced a finger down the winding crocodile tattoo on his torso, and wondered what his life might have been like if he'd bonded with a koala instead.

Shane dreamed of a wolverine.

It was a warm summer day in Stetriol, and from his vantage atop a high hill, he could see his entire kingdom.

To the north was a crumbling castle covered in cobwebs.

To the west was wasteland, flat and barren.

To the south was an abandoned village, its huts built in the Niloan style but with iron instead of wood.

To the east was the glittering sea, and upon it the looming silhouette of a great warship.

Anywhere he looked, Shane saw suffering. His eyesight was too sharp.

He removed the talisman from around his neck, and suddenly he couldn't see far at all. He could only see what was directly in front of him: a beautiful, verdant field of tall grasses and sunflowers.

And a squat, savage-looking wolverine.

"Fight me," the creature growled.

Shane realized he held a saber in his hand.

"I'm just a kid," he told the wolverine.

"Childhood is over," it said. "Fight me." And Shane realized it spoke with his uncle Gar's voice.

The wolverine leaped at him, claws and teeth shining in the sunlight. Shane went to block with his sword – and the wolverine impaled itself on the blade. Its weight and momentum pulled the sword right out of Shane's hand, and the animal fell to the ground in a bloody heap.

"I always knew you hated me," it said in Gar's voice. "I was vicious and cruel. But it was my nature. I could not help being that way."

"I'm sorry," Shane said. "I didn't mean to hurt you."

"But you hurt me anyway, Shane," Gar answered. "You killed me, whether you meant to or not. And that," he said, "is *your* nature."

The night was still and silent, but Shane jolted awake, certain that something was wrong.

He held his breath and waited for his eyes to adjust to the faint moonlight coming in through the doorway. There was no one else in the hut. He could feel his boots still beneath the straw, and knew the talismans were safe . . . for the moment.

He crept slowly to his feet, painfully so, lifting his body from the straw an inch at a time so as not to make a sound. Next he retrieved his left boot and removed the tangle of talismans, placing them in a pile on the dirt floor. The silver wolf gleamed in the moonlight. He put it on, and it was cold against his chest.

The silence of the night receded immediately. He heard an owl taking flight, the soft murmur of a stream, and a sound like chewing.

And there was the unmistakable scent of death.

Shane had been on battlefields. He knew what death smelled like. But he'd never experienced it like this before, through the heightened senses of a wolf. It was overpowering, like a physical force pressing against him, and he stumbled back, gagging. He pulled the talisman over his head and dropped it back into the pile, where it met the others with a clink of metal on metal.

Instantly the smell was gone, and Shane froze, realizing how much sound he'd just made.

There was nothing for it but to leave. Something was amiss in this village, and his sleepiness was well and truly gone.

He crammed his feet into his boots and reached for his saber, which he'd set on the bedside chest. But something stopped him from gripping the weapon – a half-remembered dream about Renneg, the wolverine he'd spent so much time pretending was his own spirit animal.

Renneg was dead now. Murdered by the Greencloaks. Conor and Rollan had almost bragged about it when they'd told him.

The sound of laughter echoed through the village.

Gooseflesh spread across Shane's skin, and this time it had nothing to do with the cool night air. He felt eyes upon him and he turned, very slowly, toward the hut's only exit.

There was a creature in the open doorway, outlined in the silver light of the moon. It looked like a large dog that had been put together all wrong. It had big, beefy shoulders and a small waist, and it stood somewhat askew. Its ears pointed off at strange angles, and it had tufts of bristly hair around its neck, like a lion's mane that had been hacked up and smeared with mud.

It made a sound like human laughter – eerily so.

The gold of Cabaro's lion caught the moonlight, and Shane lunged for it. In a single fluid motion he lifted it from the ground, dropped it around his neck, turned toward the creature, and roared.

The sound that came from his mouth was weak and high-pitched. He sounded more like a kitten than a lion.

Shane realized with a chill that he'd mistaken copper for gold in the low light.

At the same time, the creature's face came into stark relief. He could see the droplets of drool glistening from its razor-sharp teeth as it laughed again, as if genuinely mocking him.

And then the creature lunged.

Shane dodged it, and it wheeled around to keep its eyes on him from the center of the hut. He was completely cut off from his sword, the talismans were a hopeless tangle on the floor, and the space was far too small for Grahv. But now he had a clear path to the doorway. He held his fists out in front of him, trying to appear menacing, and inched sideways toward the exit.

He was still yards away when a second creature stepped through the doorway.

Shane's heart sank as the animals hooted and cackled. He could smell death again, even without the aid of Briggan's talisman. These creatures reeked of it.

He lifted his fists higher and growled. He didn't need the Golden Lion to be fearsome. And he was ready to go down fighting.

There was a sudden motion across the hut and a sharp crack, and the creature that had just stepped over the threshold yelped and crumpled to the ground. If not for the Copper Falcon around his neck, Shane would have entirely missed the small iron ball, about the size of a walnut, that had come hurtling through the open doorway and now rolled away from the animal it had knocked unconscious.

The other creature turned toward the commotion, but that was all the time it had to react before a heavy staff swung down in an arc and smashed it in the head, hammering it to the ground in a single blow.

Shane was slow to process what had happened. His eyes followed the staff back to the hands that held it – the hands of a young boy who stood in the doorway.

"Are you all right?" the boy asked.

Shane brought his fists down in relief – and then he saw the boy's eyes go wide as he got a good look at the crocodile tattoo on Shane's chest.

The boy led Shane out of the village as the first hint of dawn lightened the sky.

"Follow me," he said quietly. "It's not safe here."

"No kidding," whispered Shane. "What were those things?" He shuddered at the memory of the creatures that had attacked him – and, somehow worse, had seemed to mock him.

"Hyenas. Scavengers. I buried the people who died here, but I . . ." The boy's voice faltered. "I didn't bury them deep enough, and the hyenas found them."

Shane remembered the horrible smell, the sounds of chewing in the night. "I'm so sorry," he said. "That's awful."

"And you?" the boy said after a moment's heavy silence. He didn't look back, but Shane saw his fingers tighten on his staff. "Are you a scavenger? Come to steal from the dead?"

"No," Shane said, feigning innocence before he remembered that he was in fact innocent. "No, I was only seeking shelter from the rain. What happened here?"

"Conquerors," the boy said gravely.

Shane found he didn't have anything to say to that.

They left the clearing and walked among the trees. Shane saw evidence that the rain he'd slept through had been a heavy one. The leaves still dripped with it, and the tall grasses were so wet that his boots were soaked within moments.

The village, he decided, must have been protecting Greencloaks. It was the only explanation for the savagery with which the Conquerors had descended. Resistance in Nilo had been sporadic – in general his army was having an easier time of it than they had in Zhong. But there were those who fought back. Those who sided with the Greencloaks, even sheltered them. And those villages were dealt with harshly.

Once they'd gone a fair distance, the boy turned to face him. He was several years younger than Shane and several inches shorter than his own quarterstaff. But he handled the weapon confidently, and raised it between them now in what Shane recognized as a fighting stance.

"You're Marked," he said. "Tell me what your spirit animal is. It looked like —"

"An Amayan alligator," Shane answered flatly. He hoped the boy couldn't tell the difference between a crocodile and an alligator from a tattoo alone. Shane held his hands out at his sides, trying to look unthreatening. "I'm from Concorba," he said, remembering the name of the Amayan city where Zerif had sought out Essix.

"Every Marked person I've seen is either a Conqueror or a Greencloak." He waved his staff. "So which side are you on?"

Shane knew what the boy wanted to hear, but he couldn't bring himself to pose as a Greencloak. He decided a half-truth would serve him best. "I'm trying to stop the war," he said. "Listen . . . What's your name?"

The boy watched him suspiciously. "Achi."

"Listen, Achi. My name is Shane. Do you know why the Conquerors are here, in Nilo?"

Achi seemed uncertain. "They follow the Devourer," he said at last. "He wants to gobble up the world. He wants to rule everything."

Shane shook his head. "Not exactly. He wants the world to be free — free of the Greencloaks."

Achi narrowed his eyes, and Shane realized he was sounding an awful lot like a Conqueror.

"And the Greencloaks want . . . the Greencloaks want to protect the world, but they'll only do it on *their* terms. Both sides are so stubborn. The Conquerors are after the Greencloaks, and the Greencloaks are fighting the Conquerors, and places like Nilo get caught in the middle. What *I'm* trying to do is end this war once and for all."

"Well, good luck with that," Achi said, in a tone far too weary for a boy his age. He turned from Shane, hooked his staff through a loop in the back of his belt, and climbed the nearest tree with the grace of a cat.

Shane looked up and realized they'd been standing beneath the boy's campsite. He'd strung a hammock between two large branches, left out pots and pans to gather rainwater, and nailed a series of leather satchels around the trunk to hold the rest of his possessions.

"You don't . . . live here?" Shane asked, incredulous.

Achi gazed somberly into the distance. "I'm the village elder now," he said. "I have to keep watch." He shot Shane a patronizing look. "Lucky for you."

Shane ran his hand through his hair, brushing the bangs out of his eyes. The kid was obviously capable, but Shane couldn't leave him alone in the jungle. Could he?

"Achi." Shane sighed. "You've already done so much for me. I hate to ask for anything more, but . . . Which way to Zhong?"

Achi clucked his tongue and pointed. "That way," he said. "Like, *all* the way that way."

"I could use a guide," Shane said. "I'd make it worth your while."

Achi frowned.

"The village isn't going anywhere. And I'm way more likely to get eaten without you."

"That's true," Achi said. He considered it for a moment. "I'll take you as far as the Mumbi."

"I have no idea what that is, but it sounds fair. Oh, and Achi?" Shane flashed what he hoped was a winning smile. "Do you have anything to eat up there?"

They walked throughout the morning, stopping only briefly to stretch and share a drink from Achi's waterskin. Shane was sweating again, and he knew the heat would get worse as the day went on.

As Shane put the waterskin to his lips, Achi's eyes found the cut on his arm.

"Did the hyenas do that?" he asked.

Shane sighed. "A tree, actually."

Achi didn't smile exactly, but his eyes sparked with humor, and the seriousness seemed to lift from his features. "You can't leave a cut like that unclean. Hold on." He went off a little ways into the brush and reappeared with a thick, broad leaf shaped a bit like the blade of a short sword.

Achi bent the leaf until it snapped in two. A clear gel bled from the broken ends, which he slathered over the cut on Shane's outstretched arm. Shane felt a soothing, cooling effect almost immediately.

"See, I knew I needed your help out here," he said. "Did you learn that trick from your father?"

Achi's entire bearing changed in an instant. His shoulders tensed, his lips thinned, and his eyes went stony.

"What do you know about my father?" he asked.

"Nothing," Shane said quickly. "I just assumed . . . You said you were the village elder, and I thought maybe you were following in his footsteps."

Achi resumed applying the gel, but was considerably less delicate than before.

"I don't believe in following in anybody's footsteps," he grumbled. "And for your information, the village elder doesn't mess around with plants. He's like . . . the leader."

"Okay," Shane said, trying to sound neutral, watching as Achi discarded the leaf and fished a long cloth bandage from his bag.

"Our healer was Miss Callie. She didn't have any kids, so she taught me stuff sometimes."

Shane watched Achi as the boy looped the bandage around Shane's arm. He recognized the look of loss in the boy's eyes. It was like looking into a mirror.

"Miss Callie sounds like a wonderful person," Shane said, holding up his bandaged arm and admiring Achi's handiwork. "You honor her when you use what she taught you."

Achi's eyes softened, just a little.

Hours passed, and miles, and for Shane there was no sign that they were making any progress, just the endless indistinguishable greenery. He only knew for certain that midday had passed when Achi handed him a stick of dried meat and called it lunch.

"Why don't you let your spirit animal out?" Achi asked after a long stretch of silence.

"In this heat?" Shane responded, huffing as he followed the boy up a muddy incline. "He'd be awfully sluggish. And the terrain would trip him up."

"If I had a spirit animal, I wouldn't ever put him away."

It never ceased to amaze Shane, the way people throughout Erdas talked about spirit animals as if they were a great gift. He'd spent his entire childhood terrified of summoning one. But in the absence of bonding sickness, people celebrated the bond – and coveted it.

Most of the Marked seemed to consider their spirit animal an equal and a friend for life. Shane's bond with his own animal was much simpler. He regarded Grahv as a tool. He didn't call the creature into its active state unless he needed its muscle. Or its teeth.

But he knew what question Achi was waiting to hear, and he asked it.

"What animal do you think you'd summon?"

Achi smiled. As Shane expected, the question thrilled him. "Maybe a monkey? I like to climb."

Shane grinned. "I noticed."

"But I fight like a boar."

"A boar?"

"You saw me."

"I saw you throw a rock from a very safe distance."

"I saw *you*!" Achi countered. "Here's how Shane fights." And he flailed his arms and ran around in a tight circle, a look of mock panic on his face.

Shane laughed, a full belly laugh. Achi's sudden playfulness had caught him completely off guard.

Then Shane felt the heat of the jungle quickly recede, and a chill swept through him, starting behind his eyes and creeping down into his toes. His muscles tensed, and he felt a thoroughly unpleasant sensation in his head, as if a cold, slimy tentacle were uncoiling within his skull.

Shane's head moved of its own volition from side to side, tilted back to look up into the canopy above, then turned to regard Achi, who had drawn his quarterstaff to reenact his victory over the hyenas.

As quickly as it had begun, the episode ended. Shane felt momentarily hollowed out, like the discarded insect husks he'd seen on trees throughout the morning.

"Shane," Achi whispered.

Shane shuddered. He knew what had just happened. Gerathon had looked out from his eyes. The snake was checking up on him.

"Shane," Achi repeated, more urgently.

"Yeah," he answered, shaking his head clear. "Yes, Achi?"

"Don't panic," the boy said. "But we're being followed."

Shane tensed. "By who?"

Achi shook his head slowly, holding Shane's eyes. "Not who. It's a cat. A big one."

Shane had an impossible thought. "A cat, like . . . like a leopard?"

"Maybe," Achi answered. "I only caught a glimpse of it before it went into the trees." He inclined his head in the direction he and Shane had come from.

Shane turned. They'd been walking down a natural path through the trees, a space that was mostly free of vines and saplings. It looked almost like a tunnel, big enough for an elephant to pass through, dark with shadow except where dappled sunlight broke through the canopy.

"Hello?" Shane said, but without raising his voice.

"Shane, I don't think—"

"Abeke?" Shane called, louder this time. "Abeke, if you're out there, I can explain everything."

"Who is Abeke?" Achi whispered.

The wind stirred, and the sunlight filtering through the trees danced along the length of the tunnel. Suddenly Shane caught a glimpse of a great cat standing there, fifty yards away and right in the middle of the path, watching from the shadows.

It was not a cat he recognized. From this far away, all Shane could tell was that it was big, and as black as pitch. More like the shadow of a cat.

"Is that Abeke?" Achi whispered.

"No," Shane said, taking a step backward. "No, it's not."

"Stay calm," Achi said. "Don't run. Let's walk away nice and slowly."

Shane nodded in agreement, but kept both eyes on the large black cat.

"We're near a settlement," Achi explained in a low voice. "I was going to take us around it, but never mind that. Once the cat gets a whiff of other people, it should leave us alone." He picked up his pace, and Shane risked turning his back on the animal to follow. "In the meantime, be ready for an ambush. Keep your eyes up. If it rushes us, protect your neck—that's where the killing blow will find you."

Shane made an involuntary gurgling sound. So far he'd kept the talismans tucked away and out of sight, but now he knew he couldn't afford to pass up any advantage they gave him.

"Here," he said, holding a talisman out to Achi. "Put this on."

"Is that Uraza?" the boy asked, holding the amber cat reverently in his hands.

"A good luck charm," Shane said. If they were attacked, Achi would now find it that much easier to evade danger.

Shane, on the other hand, would go on the offensive. He looped the golden likeness of Cabaro around his own neck and unsheathed his sword, letting the sound of metal sliding against metal reverberate through the trees. "Let's keep moving."

Achi dashed ahead, his enhanced feline grace almost natural on him. The way he'd climbed the tree before, the ease with which he'd navigated the twisting maze of jungle, Shane doubted the boy would even notice the talisman's influence.

He had to increase his own pace to keep up, but that hardly seemed like a bad idea under the circumstances.

Shane was exhausted by the day's efforts. It was difficult enough to navigate the winding jungle pathways. Doubly so when keeping his guard up, never allowing his mind to wander, bracing against an attack that never came.

The light was just starting to dim when Achi finally allowed for a rest.

"We're close enough to the village that no cat will fol-low," he said. "We should camp here. But be quiet – we don't want to draw any attention."

"From the predator? Or the people?"

"Both," Achi warned.

He climbed even more nimbly now that he wore Abeke's talisman – *Uraza's talisman*, Shane corrected himself. In no time, Achi had strung his hammock in the tree, high enough that any passing patrol would miss it entirely – not to mention ants, boars, snakes, and many other creatures that could do them harm in the night.

Shane clambered up after him.

"I'm sorry I don't have a spare," Achi said. "But we should probably sleep in shifts anyway."

"What's in that village that has you so spooked?"

"Conquerors," he answered. "And worse."

Shane startled. This was a stroke of luck. Of course, he realized, he should have been seeking out Conquerors all along. He didn't have to travel all the way back to camp on foot. He could walk right into that village, eat and drink like . . . well, like a king . . . and ride out tomorrow on a fast horse with a full complement of soldiers at his back.

But it would be difficult to convince Achi they were better off in the village than up a tree.

"Conquerors and worse," Shane echoed. "What do you mean?"

"Never mind," Achi said, turning away. "I'm tired."

"I'll take first watch, then," Shane offered, giving up, for the moment, thoughts of a hot meal.

Achi crawled into his makeshift bed and Shane climbed higher, finding a branch just below the canopy that was large enough to bear his weight. Before he'd even settled in, though, he heard a whisper from below.

"Shane. Hey, Shane."

Shane peered down. "Yes, Achi?"

"Can you tell me a story?"

"I thought you were tired," Shane said, but when Achi made no reply, he felt a pang of guilt. "Hold on," he said, and he made his way back down to the hammock.

"It's been a while since I heard a story," Achi said. "Miss Callie used to tell me them sometimes." He sounded far younger than the gruff, serious boy of just minutes ago.

"I don't really know any stories," Shane said. "None with happy endings."

"They don't have any legends where you're from?"

Shane thought about it. "Oh, I know," he said. "Did you ever hear the story about how the goanna and the perentie got their coloring?"

"The what and the who?" Achi said. Even in the gloom, Shane caught his skeptical look.

"Right," Shane said, remembering he was supposed to be from Amaya anyway. "Why don't you tell me a story, then? A story about Nilo?"

Achi lifted the amber talisman from his chest and then looked at the one Shane wore. "Uraza and Cabaro," he said. "Did you know they're the reason gorillas don't have tails?"

"I didn't know that," said Shane. "Tell me about it."

Long ago, when Erdas was young, the Great Beasts had not yet grown into their greatness. Uraza was little more

than a kitten, and Cabaro had no mane. Yet they both had claws, and they bared them over Nilo.

Nilo, you see, was the most beautiful of all the lands, rich in game and lush in climate. Each of the cats wished to claim it as their own.

They bickered for many days, yowling and hissing and clawing at the ground, and the land around them suffered. For even in their youth, the cats were powerful, and wherever their mighty claws tore up the grass, nothing new would grow. Thus were the Niloan deserts formed.

Kovo saw this, and he was worried, for he also called Nilo his home. He knew he would not thrive in the desert, and so he sought a way to end their fighting.

First he went to Cabaro. He flattered the cat's vanity. "You are stronger than Uraza," Kovo cooed. "But true strength is in numbers. You must gather others of your kind, and work together to claim Nilo."

Then Kovo went to Uraza. He appealed to the cat's pride. "You are faster and more agile than Cabaro," he said. "You will control Nilo if you remain a solitary hunter and strike from the trees."

And then there was a time of peace. Cabaro and his lionesses stayed on the savannah, in plain sight, relying on their strength and on teamwork. But there were too many of them to move freely through the jungles. Uraza, by contrast, ruled the trees, relying on stealth and skill and staying well clear of the savannah.

Each had their own place, and so there was no longer any reason to fight over Nilo. Yet the cats came to realize that they had been tricked into their truce, and they did not take kindly to this. They chased Kovo up into the *mountains, and finally caught him by his long and beautiful tail. Kovo escaped, but he lost the tail to the cats.*

"That is what you get for sticking your tail into a cat's business," they said.

And from that day forth, Cabaro and Uraza lived in harmony. The leopard called the forests and jungles of Nilo her home, for she was a great climber, and the trees became her hunting ground. The lion ruled over the savannah, for his might was such that he feared no enemy, and he had no need for stealth or hiding.

⌁⌁⌁

Shane chuckled softly. "And to this day, I'd bet Kovo holds a grudge," he added. He tried to imagine what the great gorilla would think of such a legend. He doubted he'd be flattered—but then, at least his cunning had been immortalized.

Within a minute, Achi's breathing slowed, and Shane crept quietly back to a higher branch. He swapped out the talisman he wore, surveying their surroundings with Essix's sight, but as the night grew darker the talisman grew less useful.

He tried Kovo's again, spurred on by the legend he'd just heard. As he remembered, it sharpened his vision. But the effect was not at all like that of the Copper Falcon. Again his eyes were drawn to the stress points of the branches—the one he sat upon seemed to glow right at its base, where his weight caused it to strain against the tree. He looked down at Achi, and even in the dark he could see details of the boy: the delicate bones of his fingers, his eyes in their sockets, a cluster of nerves at the base of his skull.

Shane felt suddenly sick. He knew exactly what the talisman allowed him to see: weakness.

It was showing him how best to hurt Achi.

Shane removed the pendant. It was darker than the night itself. No moonlight caught its curved surface. He put it away, and opted for Briggan's heightened hearing instead.

The jungle came alive at night, but if anything stalked them, he could not find any sign of it. They did get one visitor, however. Several hours into his vigil, Shane caught a musky scent and heard something small and agile moving in the branches of an adjacent tree. Eventually a monkey peered curiously at him through a curtain of leaves. Its face was black, and the fur of its body appeared almost green. It made a chittering sound, which Shane imagined was a greeting.

"*Shh,*" he hushed, then pointed to Achi. "He's sleeping."

The monkey cocked its head quizzically. Shane thought it would make a perfect spirit animal for Achi. He suddenly remembered the Bile in his pocket. He drew the vial and considered the amber liquid within.

This, he realized, *could* be perfect. Achi could have the spirit animal he wanted. Shane could win him over to the Conquerors' cause, giving the boy a home and a purpose. He might hesitate at first — might resist accepting that the soldiers had done what had to be done in his village. But that was the beauty of the Bile, wasn't it? No one could resist it in the end.

Not even stubborn, foolhardy Drina.

Shane frowned, a chill spreading up his back. Before he could reconsider, he quickly unstopped the vial and poured out its contents.

He was a king. A commander of armies. He didn't need to bribe Achi, and he didn't need to bully him either.

As if the boy knew Shane was weighing his fate, he began to toss and turn in his sleep. He cried out into the night, and swayed so much that Shane feared he might launch himself right out of the hammock.

Shane climbed back down to Achi and shook him gently on the shoulder.

"Achi," he said. "It's only a dream."

Achi opened his eyes. They glistened with wetness.

"What is it?" Shane asked.

Achi shook his head. All his flintiness was gone. It had been gone since they'd set up camp.

"It has to do with the village, doesn't it? The one nearby."

Achi was silent a moment, then let out a shuddering sigh. "It's not just Conquerors down there," Achi said. "My dad's with them."

"They took him?" Shane asked. "Is he a prisoner? I can get him—"

"No," Achi said. "He's *with* them. He . . . he was the elder of our village, like you guessed. He was in charge. Everybody did whatever he said. Everybody trusted him.

"When the Conquerors came, my dad went out to meet them. I snuck out and followed him and listened. They wanted him to turn over our Greencloak. The one who provides Nectar at our ceremonies, they said. But we didn't *have* a Greencloak in our village. There was a woman who brought the Nectar once a year, but we never saw her at other times."

Achi took a deep breath. "They didn't believe him. They thought he was protecting someone. They got violent. And then he . . . he told them he was sorry. That he had lied, and that there *was* a Greencloak in our village. He offered to lead them right to her."

Shane felt a sourness in the pit of his stomach.

"He brought them to the village and walked them right up to Miss Callie's hut. She was no Greencloak. She wasn't even Marked. But the Conquerors pulled her from her home. Everyone got upset. They came out to help her. They threw rocks and shouted. But the Conquerors . . ." His voice broke. "The Conquerors had armor and real weapons. In the end, they got what they wanted. And my dad went right along with them."

Shane was struck dumb by the senseless horror of Achi's story. Before he could think of a single thing to say, the boy burst into tears. Sobs racked his small body, swaying the hammock from side to side.

With some effort, Shane crawled in alongside him. He held Achi until his tears ran dry, murmuring that it was okay, that everything would work out, and wondering whether this was his biggest lie yet.

Shane dreamed of a jackal.

It sat upon an iron throne.

In its jaws was a bloody golden crown, forged in the shape of a snake devouring its own tail.

Shane awoke with surprise at the first hint of dawn. He was wedged into the hammock. Achi was crouched on a branch above him.

"I fell asleep," Shane said groggily.

Achi shrugged. "I kept watch." There was no sign of sorrow on the boy's face, as if he'd left his worries in the dark.

Shane slid to the ground and stretched while Achi gathered the hammock. He still wore Uraza's talisman. Shane could have believed it gave the boy claws—he clung to the side of the tree so effortlessly.

Achi leaped to the ground from a height that Shane wouldn't have dared. He landed on his feet, of course.

"Ready to go?" he asked, so much enthusiasm in his voice that it broke Shane's heart a little.

"Listen, Achi . . ."

"I gathered some grubs while you slept. For breakfast!" Achi held out a closed fist, and Shane had no desire to see what it contained.

"I'm going to the village, Achi," he said soberly. "And I think you should come with me."

Achi's smile snapped closed like a bear trap.

"I know you're angry with your father," Shane said. "And you have every right to be. What he did was wrong. But listen . . ." He squatted down and put a hand on Achi's shoulder. "It's like the story you told me about Kovo. Remember? Kovo lied, but he did it for a good reason. He got the cats to stop fighting. He saved the day!"

Achi gave him a withering look. "Kovo was *not* the hero of that story."

"Wasn't he?" Shane said. "Achi, the thing you have to understand is this: Sometimes good people do bad things. It doesn't mean they're bad people."

"That's exactly what it means!" Achi hollered.

"You need to forgive your father," Shane said forcefully. "He was doing what he thought was right for the village and for—"

Achi shoved Shane, hard, and he skidded into the dirt.

Shane could hardly believe it had happened. He was torn between shock, hurt, and anger—and then he saw the shaft of an arrow sticking out from a tree.

Right where his head had been.

"Shane, run!" Achi shouted.

They dashed into the trees, and Shane struggled to swap talismans while keeping his head down. He didn't need Briggan's hearing to catch the dramatic crashing behind him as something large and fast moved toward them through the brush.

He needed the lion.

Shane skidded to a stop, twirled on his heel, and roared.

The sound was so great it was a physical force, pushing at the trees like a hurricane so that they bent low to the ground. One of them snapped in half, its thick trunk reduced to splinters. Despite the countless leaves and twigs that flew into the air, blocking Shane's vision, he easily saw the huge cat that had been charging them. It hurtled backward in the gale, sliding through the mud. Even as it tumbled away, the fierceness in its eyes and the savage points of its teeth gave Shane chills.

He turned to find Achi had stopped to look at him. "What was–?"

"Run!" Shane said.

He didn't mean to.

He just didn't think.

But his shouted warning came out as another great wave of crushing force.

Achi flew.

All that mattered now was speed.

When Shane retrieved the talisman from Achi's unconscious body, the boy's head lolled back and his arms hung limply. He'd flown high, come down hard, and was now out cold, his shallow breathing the only evidence that he was still alive.

Shane took the boy in his arms, donned the Amber Leopard, and ran. He fought the urge to look behind him, to see if the black cat had recovered and resumed its pursuit.

He felt a calmness overtake him. To be running through the jungle suddenly felt like the most natural thing in the world. He no longer had to even think about where he was placing his feet, or which way to turn to avoid the low branches and hanging curtains of vines. He was a wild thing, running free. He was Uraza, and he was home.

But he was not alone.

Just ahead, a solitary figure stepped out from between the trees. Her cloak was green, but so dark as to appear almost black. Its hood obscured her face. She had an arrow nocked in her bow, and she was aiming it right at him.

"Devourer," she said. "We meet at last."

Shane skidded to a stop.

"I'll bet you thought you'd escaped for good," the woman said. "Once from Greenhaven and then from the ship that pursued you. I'll admit, it was an interesting chase. But I saw you fall from the eagle."

"This boy needs a healer," Shane said sternly.

"That boy is a shield to you." She pulled her bowstring taut. "Put him down. Die with some dignity."

Shane ground his teeth. "I get it. You don't like me much. But I'm telling you, if this boy doesn't get to a healer right now, what happens is on your head."

The woman took a step forward, and Shane saw her face beneath the hood. Her tan skin and accent marked her as a native of southern Zhong. For all the malice in her voice, her features were expressionless, her eyes flat. She had flecks of gray in her black hair and a tattoo on her arm, a white tiger, but it was faded away almost to nothing.

"You use the talismans well," she said.

"Thanks," Shane said. "I'd curtsy, but my hands are full."

"The lion's roar. The leopard's grace," she continued. "Tell me, if you're so concerned for the child's life, why not call on the panda?"

Shane cursed himself. It hadn't even occurred to him. Not that it would have been a very strategic choice with a man-eating cat bearing down on him.

"You care only for yourself." The woman seethed, her stony exterior flaring hot now. "My name is Lishay. I lost my brother to your pet monsters. I lost my spirit animal. And I lost the man I – a good man. Tarik."

"I haven't killed anyone," Shane growled.

"So talented a liar," Lishay said. "You can even lie to yourself."

"I'm not –"

"You may not have held the greatsword that struck Tarik down. Nor the knife that took my kin. But make no mistake – you are responsible for their deaths and more. Your crocodile killed the greatest general in Zhong. *You* unleashed this madness upon Erdas."

"I've lost people too!" Shane shouted, spittle flying from his mouth. "You think you're special? I'm doing this because *you're* the monsters. Greencloaks! You left Stetriol to rot!" Shane spit into the dirt. "So high and mighty. Not against sending an assassin after me, though, are they?"

"Put the boy down," she said. "Last chance." And Shane caught her glimpsing over his shoulder.

"Grahv!" he called, and he rolled to the side just as the great black cat lunged from behind him. It was a tiger, he saw now, its stripes almost lost entirely against its dark fur.

The crocodile appeared in a flash and met the tiger mid-lunge, allowing Shane to bring his attention back to Lishay just as she let the arrow fly. With Uraza's speed, he was able to dodge it, but only barely. He needed to end this fight quickly.

He dropped Achi to the ground, pivoted, and pulled his saber as he closed the distance.

She met him with a parry, catching his sword on her

bow and pushing it aside even as she drew a curved blade with her free hand.

Shane leaped back, dodging the slash she aimed at his belly. He brought his sword around for a slash of his own, and metal met metal.

For the moment, it was a stalemate. Their eyes met, and if a look of hate were a physical thing, Shane would have been knocked off his feet.

They were too evenly matched. Shane needed an advantage.

He withdrew, walking backward but keeping his sword before him. Then he leaped into a tree, out of Lishay's reach.

She sheathed her sword, and Shane knew he had mere moments before she let an arrow fly. He acted quickly, and replaced the Amber Leopard with Kovo's Obsidian Ape.

Shane could see an old injury in the woman's wrist, a fresh scrape on her cheek, and little else he could exploit while her guard was up.

But the black tiger lit up like a beacon. Shane knew she must love the animal fiercely – Kovo's pendant had flagged it as her weakness. Could he help Grahv get the upper hand? He turned to look at the tiger, and that's when he noticed something that nearly stunned him right out of the tree: Achi was lit up as well.

Despite her earlier bluster, the woman didn't want harm to come to the child.

And *that* was something Shane could use.

Shane ducked and weaved through the branches, hoping she didn't have a bead on him yet, but unable to take his eyes away from his hands and feet for fear of falling. "Grahv!" he shouted. "The boy!"

Their mental link sparked, and Shane could feel it as the crocodile rallied, knocking the tiger aside with his massive tail and turning on Achi. In a burst of speed, the crocodile had Achi in his open mouth.

"I'm coming down!" Shane said. "Lower your bow if you value the boy's life."

Shane clambered down the tree to find Lishay standing stock-still. The only weapon she had now was hatred, which she radiated at him.

"Call off the tiger," Shane said, drawing his sword.

She hesitated, but held out her arm. In a flash of light, the black tiger appeared as a tattoo alongside its white cousin.

Black and white. Precisely how the Greencloaks saw the world.

"You're a monster," she spat. "And you'll pay. If not at my hands, then at another's."

"I've paid in advance," Shane said. "Now it's time I collect my due."

With Kovo's sight to guide him, he smashed the pommel of his sword into the base of her skull. She dropped to the ground, instantly unconscious.

But the jungle wasn't quiet. Shane heard the sound of crying, and turned to see that Achi was awake. Awake, and terrified.

"Achi, it's okay," Shane said quickly. "Grahv won't hurt you."

In a flash, the crocodile disappeared.

But the fear in Achi's eyes remained.

Shane staggered into the village as the dawn sky flared amber and violet, as if Uraza's colors still flew over Nilo.

But Nilo had fallen to the Conquerors, and in this village, Uraza's flags had been replaced.

A dozen Conquerors leveled their weapons at him as he stepped forward. A dozen spirit animals bared their teeth. Shane wondered if they'd really attack him while he held an injured boy in his arms, then decided he'd rather not know the answer.

Grahv appeared growling beside him, and soldiers and animals alike recoiled.

"Send out your captain," he commanded. "And the elder from the village you destroyed. Now!"

The captain appeared in the doorway of the nearest hut, the medals of his station gleaming in the early light. He hastened over, eyes on the crocodile. "On your knees, dogs!" he shouted at his men. "You are in the presence of royalty." He removed his iron helm and bowed his head. "Forgive them, my liege, but we were not expecting you."

"Achi!" called a man, and Shane looked up to see a middle-aged Niloan man approaching. He held a staff much like the one Achi cherished. Shane hadn't even thought to retrieve it when the boy had fallen.

The man paid no heed to Grahv, nor the soldiers. He walked right up to Shane, worry etched across his brow. "Achi, are you all right? What happened?"

"Answer your father, Achi," Shane prompted.

Achi glared at Shane. His eyes had gone stony again. Shane had given him Jhi's talisman and carried him all the way here despite the ache in his limbs. But Achi had refused to speak the entire way.

Shane handed him over to his father, careful to reclaim the bamboo pendant first. "He got caught in the middle of a fight. A Greencloak ambushed us in the woods. But he'll be okay."

Shane turned to the captain. "You're responsible for the wrecked village west of here?"

"Yes, my king," the captain said. "We met resistance there, but we overcame it." There was pride in his voice.

Shane slapped him across the face.

"Idiot," he seethed. "Those were innocent people." The soldiers all around him fidgeted uncomfortably. "Captain, you will return to the village – alone – and you will dig proper graves for those people." The man stood at attention, acknowledging the order in stunned silence. "And I'd suggest you hurry. You really want to finish before dark."

As the captain trotted off, Shane turned to Achi and winked, but the boy seemed unmoved.

Achi's father cleared his throat. "Achi. This great man saved you. Carried you to safety. You should show gratitude. He is a hero!"

Achi scowled. "Sometimes bad people do good things," he said icily. "It doesn't mean they're good people."

Shane said nothing, just watched as Achi was carried away.

He tried to grasp at a fleeting sensation of victory, but it slipped through his fingers and was gone.

PART 3
VENGEANCE

*"What if you had been me?"
Shane pressed on. "What if
you were the crown prince of
an island prison—a nation
condemned by the
Greencloaks for the crimes
of their ancestors? What
would you do?"*

*—Spirit Animals:
Book 7:* The Evertree

THE STREETS OF CLAROBO WERE ALIVE WITH CELEBRA-
tion. Men and women danced in the boulevards, their
voices mixing with the sounds of musical instruments
and sizzling meat and laughing children. Birds circled and
sang in the skies above, spirit animals riding the wave
of joy they sensed in their partners. There were people
in costume, wearing the colorful plumage of tropical
birds, or face paint in the likeness of pandas or leopards
or wolves. There were jugglers, and a man on stilts, and
a woman who ate fire before a crowd of enraptured
onlookers.

The entire town, it seemed, had come out to celebrate
the defeat of the Conquerors.

"Yeah, yeah. We get it," Shane muttered to himself.
"You won. We lost. Do you have to rub it in?"

He knew sulking wouldn't help him fit in, but he
couldn't manage to force a smile. The wounds of his defeat
were still raw. As he watched, a crowd at one end of the
street gathered around a stuffed crocodile and a scarecrow dressed to resemble a man in silver and black armor:
the Devourer.

He wasn't surprised when they set the straw dummies
on fire, but he was astonished by the intensity in their
voices as they cheered the flames. There was real hatred
there. Real hunger for revenge.

Shane hiked up the hood of his cloak. He knew no one
would recognize him here. Most people didn't have any

idea that the Devourer they so reviled was just a boy. But he wasn't taking any chances.

Zhong had been left a smoldering wreck in the wake of the Conquerors' invasion. Nilo had seen entire villages destroyed, and Eura's great forests had been trampled and torched as the armies marched west. Amaya's capital had been taken, but Clarobo had escaped the ravages of war. Its people had spent months preparing for an attack. Now they knew that attack would never come. Clarobo had been spared, and tonight, she celebrated.

Everything about the place was bright. Bright costumes, bright lanterns, bright smiles. But Shane knew that shadows thrive where light shines brightest. There would be people among the crowd who were not here to celebrate, but to take advantage of the gathering. And those were the people Shane needed to find.

He did not have to wait long. As he leaned against the wall of a house and watched, a boy with a dirty face and quick fingers lifted the contents of a woman's pocket. The boy continued walking along nonchalantly, almost blending into the crowd before Shane could react.

But Shane dodged among the revelers, using all the grace he'd honed on the battlefield. On instinct, his fingers itched to reach for his saber, but he squashed the feeling and left the blade concealed beneath his heavy cloak.

Instead he let his fingers find the boy, gripping him by the shoulder and pulling him aside.

"What's the matter?" the boy asked, making his eyes big, trying to look even younger than he was.

"Don't play innocent with me," Shane countered. "I

wrote the book on *that* particular trick. And I saw what you did back there."

The boy tugged free of Shane's grip but stood his ground. "Fine, take it," he said, shoving something small and warm into Shane's hands. "I don't want any trouble."

Shane was expecting money, or one of the jeweled charms of Essix so popular in the region. But that wasn't what he found himself holding.

"You stole roasted nuts?"

The boy shrugged. "They smell good."

Shane looked the boy over more closely. He was wearing old, ill-fitting clothing, and the dirt wasn't just on his face, but caked in his fingernails. He tossed the bag of nuts back, and the boy caught them easily.

"I'm not trying to get you in trouble. I was just hoping you might give me directions."

"Directions?" the boy asked, perplexed. "Why ask me?"

"Because I need to find the kinds of places the bright, happy people don't go," Shane clarified, pointing a thumb over his shoulder as a boar-faced reveler twirled past.

"I might know my way around," the boy said. "But my memory's real bad when I'm hungry." Then he wagged his eyebrows.

Shane sighed, digging a coin from his pocket. "I need to know where people go for . . ." He lowered his voice as he handed the coin over. "Potions. Poisons. That sort of thing."

The boy pursed his lips. "There's a lot of places like that," he said.

"I've been to several," Shane said. "Take me to one I wouldn't have found on my own."

"If you say so," the boy said, and Shane followed him off the bright street and down a twisting warren of alleyways. Here, Shane could relax a little. He took down his hood as the sounds of laughter and music faded away.

The boy brought him to an unmarked door. "This is it," he said.

"Thanks." Shane considered the coins in his pocket. He had no way of knowing how much money he would need. He'd come to Amaya for revenge, and revenge could be costly.

But he could always get more money.

The boy's eyes widened again, this time in genuine delight, as Shane handed over the entire contents of his coin purse.

"Don't spend it all on carnival food," he warned. "Get something nutritious." The boy skipped away down the alley, headed back toward the bustling crowds. "And if you see anyone wearing a green cloak out there," Shane called after him, "kick them in the shins for me!"

The space was cramped and dark, and its smell was unlike anything Shane had encountered before – or perhaps more accurately, its smell was like everything he'd encountered before, all at once. There was incense and the reek of newly flowering plants, scented reeds, and cooking herbs, and the musk of unseen animals. Dried plants hung from the rafters, with living specimens springing up from pots placed on shelves and along the baseboards and even in the middle of the slanted wooden floor. But what drew

Shane's eye were the frogs. There were dozens of them interspersed among the plants, all huddled in glass containers and grouped by color.

And what colors! Red and silver, blue and yellow, bright pink, and a green the shade of a Niloan oasis. They gleamed like jewels in the gloom of the shop.

Among the dazzling array, one frog stood out—a solitary golden specimen, alone in its jar upon a low shelf. It had one glossy black eye fixed on Shane and remained perfectly still aside from its throat, which moved rhythmically in time with its breathing. Shane tapped at the glass with his finger.

"Very deadly, that one," said a voice, and Shane whirled to see that a woman had appeared from behind a curtained doorway. Her face was lined with age but gave no hint of emotion.

"Deadly?" Shane echoed. "A frog?"

"Dangerous things can come in small packages, child," she said, lifting an eyebrow. "Present company included, I think. Or am I to believe you stumbled upon my shop by accident?"

"Not by accident, no," he answered, puffing out his chest a bit. "But I'm not here for a pet."

Shane kept his gaze upon the woman's face as he withdrew an item from his cloak pocket: a small vial of amber-colored liquid.

He saw the flash of recognition in her eyes. "You know what this is," he said. Not a question.

"It's nothing," she spat. "Useless. Get out of my shop."

"Peace, madam," he said, holding up his hand. "I suspect we have an enemy in common."

She regarded him coolly. "Go on."

"I'm tracking a woman. She's old, and she's crafty. She was last seen boarding a ship to Clarobo with little but the clothes on her back – and several vials of this liquid. I thought she might try to sell it when she docked."

"She didn't sell it, but she made a trade," the woman said. "She claimed this liquid was the secret to the Conquerors' success." She frowned. "Mind you, this was before word reached us that the Conquerors weren't very successful in the end."

"They came close, though," Shane said, fighting to keep his voice steady.

"Of course they did. They say every man and woman in their army had a spirit animal. Can you imagine? Too many of them to be a coincidence. And I don't much believe in fate. Which leaves one other possibility."

Shane allowed her a dramatic pause.

"I think perhaps someone found a way to change the rules." She took the vial from his hand. "We've all heard the rumors here. That the Conquerors had their own form of Nectar. They called it Bile, and it was even more powerful than the variety the Greencloaks have hoarded so jealously over the years. It would be worth a fortune." She uncorked the vial and sniffed. How she could make out a single scent among all the others in the shop, Shane had no idea. "This is the very substance I got from the crone. You're right – she was crafty. She claimed to have no knowledge of it other than that it was taken from a Conqueror camp. She knew I would assume it was the Bile, that I would think it was *I* taking advantage of *her*." She snorted. "I have fed it to animals and to children. I have poured it over plants, boiled it, frozen it, and brewed it into a distressingly bitter tea. Indeed, bitterness appears to be its only notable quality: both bitterness of flavor, and the bitterness of disappointment it brought me." She poured the vial's contents out onto the floor.

Shane frowned. "I wasn't quite done with that."

"You're in luck." The woman cackled, bending beneath the counter and producing a box full of identical stoppered vials of liquid. "We have a surplus!"

Shane whistled. "That would make a lot of tea. What did she ask for in return?"

"A small thing. An antitoxin."

"What?" Shane frowned. "Was she sick?"

The woman shrugged. "She did not appear so. Yet she requested the antidote for a particular venom found in a particular snake that lives in the jungle west of here."

"The jungle?" Shane muttered. "What could she possibly . . . What sort of snake?"

"The bushmaster." She threw up her hands. "More than that, I do not know."

"She's gone into the jungle," Shane said. "Okay." He picked up the box of Bile. "Can I take this? It might help me track her."

The woman's forehead crinkled. "How would it—?"

The box slipped through Shane's fingers, crashing to the ground, the vials shattering all around his boots. "I'm so sorry!" he said.

"Idiot!" the woman shouted. "You're lucky that was nothing valuable. Out! Out before you do real damage."

Shane apologized again as he fled from the shop,

ducking his head as if embarrassed. Really, he was hiding a smile.

The Bile was useless. That was true. It had been a key part of Gerathon's plan, and now Gerathon was dead. Shane had seen the Great Serpent destroyed with his own eyes. Her talisman was gone, too, and with it, every last drop of the Bile had lost its power. But what if it didn't stay that way? What if it could somehow do more harm?

The Bile was Shane's mess. And he was looking to clean up his messes.

Even if that means making a few new ones, he mused, and he wiped the amber slime from his boots.

Shane realized he was being followed a few minutes after leaving the poisoner's lair.

He wanted to believe it was just paranoia. Being the leader of a disgraced and defeated army, and possibly the most hated person in Erdas, he could be forgiven for being on edge. But as he wove through the darkened alleyways, plunged into the light of the festival, stopped to trade for a bag of roasted nuts (they really did smell good), then turned off the main strip again, he continuously caught sight of a cloaked figure in his peripheral vision.

Had he been recognized?

There was nothing to do but confront his pursuer. Anything less, and he risked the person finding reinforcements or calling the authorities. Shane hadn't technically broken any laws, but he'd seen what the crowd had done to that scarecrow earlier. There were plenty of people in

Clarobo who believed Shane was committing a crime just by breathing.

He took a left turn, and a right, and a left. He picked up his pace, forcing the cloaked figure to do the same. But as he turned a final corner, rather than speed up in an attempt to shake pursuit, he stopped running, drew his sword, and waited.

A young woman came around the corner moments later. She saw him, saw his sword, and skidded to a stop.

"It's not what you think," she said, holding up her hands. "I want to help you."

Shane kept his saber up. "You sound just like a snake I used to know. Pull your hood down."

She did as he directed, and Shane could barely make out her features in the low light of the alleyway. She was a stranger, with dark hair cut short, sharp cheekbones, and fierce, unafraid eyes. "My name is Anya. I heard you speaking with my mistress back at the shop. I wished to see if you would really go into the jungle alone."

"What's it matter to you?"

"It is too dangerous. I spend a great deal of time there."

"In the jungle?"

She nodded.

"Why is that?"

The girl bit her lower lip. "The mistress's frogs. It is my job to collect them."

Shane lowered his sword, but he left it unsheathed. "I'm going into the jungle. If you have any advice for me – other than 'don't do that' – I'm happy to listen."

"At least wait until morning. To go now would be a terrible mistake."

Shane sighed. "I know. I was hoping to hire a guide, in fact."

"I am going tomorrow, in the afternoon. I could walk with you a short way. Show you the paths." She looked him up and down. "A boy who pursues a woman across the sea in fine boots can afford my services, I'm sure."

"I'm sure," Shane echoed. "But in that case, you work for me. And we're leaving at dawn."

"Very well," Anya said. "But I must ask: Who is this woman to you, that you would follow her across the world?"

"Her name is Yumaris," he answered, sheathing his saber. "She used to be my tutor."

Anya laughed. "Your teacher has left you, and you follow her now for your next lesson?"

"No, I'm following her because she killed my sister," Shane said coldly. "And this time, I'm the one who will be teaching the lesson."

"What separates man from beast?"

The question had stumped Shane as a child. He remembered sitting in Yumaris's stuffy stone chamber within Stetriol's castle, trying to puzzle out the answer.

He hated his tutor's room, and he wasn't much fonder of the woman herself. Yumaris was ancient and humorless, with a dry, rasping voice and sour breath. She complained endlessly of a chill draft in the castle, one only she seemed to feel, and every day she piled a heavy, ratty, hooded cloak over her bony frame, letting it drag behind her as she shuffled along the corridors. She hung thick curtains over her windows, trapping the stale, warm air within her chamber. The curtains blocked out sunlight, too, so all Shane's lessons were delivered by candlelight, no matter the time of day.

And it was impossible to predict what those lessons would be. More than once he had stayed up all night reading about some key event in Stetriolan history, only to have Yumaris ignore the assignment entirely and lecture him for hours about rocks.

As Shane's parents and sister grew sicker, he was left entirely to her whims.

And she seemed to take a twisted pleasure in stumping him.

"What separates man from beast?" she asked him, out of nowhere, while he was trying to concentrate on a sheet of math problems.

He gave her a blank look.

"What distinguishes a human from an animal?" she asked. "What makes us different?"

Shane sighed and put down his pencil. When Yumaris veered down a path, he had no choice but to follow . . . however much he wanted to stand up, knock her aside, and run from the dark, musty room into the springtime outside.

"Restraint?" he guessed.

She gestured with her hand for him to say more.

"When an animal wants to do something, it does it." He imagined tearing the curtains down on his way out the door, hurling them into a fire. "But humans worry about . . . good behavior. About following the rules."

Yumaris shook her head. "Does the crocodile who waits hours for the right opportunity to strike not show restraint?" she asked. "Does the pack of wolves showing deference to their alpha male not display respect for the rules of their little society? Try again."

Shane huffed. He thought about animals, and his mind went to his sister's monstrous spider. Every day Magda swept the creature's webs away from the corners of the castle, and every day the spider rewove them, seemingly unbothered.

"Humans can learn. We learn and grow and change in ways an animal can't."

"Hmm," Yumaris said, tapping her wrinkled chin with one gnarled finger. "I suppose we had best tell your father's hound master that he wastes his time training dogs to hunt and heel, since it seems they will never learn from him. And the falconer, and the stablemen . . ."

"All right," Shane said, fully annoyed. "I yield. What is the answer you're looking for?"

Yumaris smiled, showing her crooked yellow teeth. "Tools."

Shane mimicked her hand gesture from before, inviting her to expand upon her answer.

"A bird may build a nest, but it will never do so with hammer or hatchet or saw. Ape may fight ape for territory, but they will never do so with weapons forged of iron."

"Lucky for the apes," Shane said.

"Well," said Yumaris, "I suppose that's a matter of perspective." And then she went silent and paced about the room. Shane assumed she meant for him to return to his math assignment. But just as he'd taken up his pencil, Yumaris spoke again.

"What separates king from commoner?"

Shane sensed a trick question. There were too many ways to answer. Did Yumaris expect him to show humility? Pride?

In the end he merely shrugged.

"A castle is not built by a king," Yumaris said. "Oh, he has hammers and hatchets aplenty. But he also has men and women to toil with them on his behalf. Likewise, a war is not fought by a king. It is fought by the king's subjects, who act as his shield and his sword." She smiled once more. "The answer is: tools. A king has better tools." Her smile deepened. "Some of them are people."

The inns were packed while the festival was in full swing, but Shane found a ramshackle tavern with a room full of cots in the back. He traded his fancy belt buckle for a cot for the night and a bowl of stew he had little appetite for. The luxuries of his childhood seemed very far away. The castle in Stetriol had never seemed opulent. It was dusty and drafty and full of aging, threadbare furniture. But he'd always had a bed, and clean clothes, and a hot meal any time he wanted. If this year of war had taught him anything, it was how much he'd taken for granted as a prince.

He hardly slept for all the snoring and the movement of people coming and going throughout the night. The shuttered window did little to block out the sounds of celebration, and Shane's mind raced with all the possibilities the next day might bring. Before he knew it, it was dawn.

The streets were still not empty, with pockets of revelers clustered in loud groups. Trash was everywhere. *This is what people do with their freedom*, thought Shane. *While Zhong is in ruins, the people of Amaya cheer their own good fortune.*

But then, here he was, with no idea how the people of Stetriol fared without him.

Anya met him right where she'd promised, on the outskirts of town, dressed in green fabric and brown leather. She had a bow and a quiver full of arrows, and flasks of water hung from her backpack. It made Shane realize just how unprepared he was.

"After you," he said.

The town was not built right at the edge of the jungle. An acre of farmland stood between them and the wall of trees in the distance.

"This is the easy part of our journey," Anya said after a stretch of silence. "The jungle terrain is more difficult and far more dangerous."

"Is it very different from the forests of Nilo? I've spent some time there."

Anya had a very expressive face, and she made a show of her surprise at this news. "You have been to Nilo? I would like to see it. But as I understand it, our woodlands are different. There, the people live within the forest. They are able to build there, and find food, and live . . . if not in harmony with nature, then in a state of truce."

Shane nodded, remembering the burned-out village where he'd attempted to stay the night. It had been overrun with vicious hyenas—but only after soldiers had wrecked it.

"Our jungle is not a peaceful place," Anya warned.

"The snakes are venomous. The fish have teeth to rival the jaguars'." She smiled grimly at him as they approached the tree line. "Even the frogs can kill a person. Here, everything is out to get you."

"I'll keep that in mind," Shane said glumly. "And if I feel the need to pet anything, I'll check with you first."

Anya's laugh tinkled as she pulled a machete from her bag and set to hacking away the first of the vines. She quickly disappeared into the shrouded twilight beneath the trees, and Shane took a deep breath and plunged in after her.

The heat was far worse than it had been in Nilo. The air was so thick that Shane imagined he could hack at it with Anya's machete, and the blade would come away warm and wet. But they had plenty of water, and fruit and dried meats, and it was an altogether less harrowing experience than his trek across Nilo had been.

After about an hour, Shane asked, "Are there any structures out here? Old forts?"

Anya wiped at her brow. "Several old temples. There is one nearby. Long abandoned. I have only seen it once — people think it's cursed."

"That's where we want to go."

"Truly?" Anya kept hacking at vines as she spoke. "I thought you wished to see a bushmaster snake. They are most common somewhat south of there."

"The woman I'm tracking is clever. 'Bushmaster' is a code. And it leads to that jungle temple."

"Does she wish to be found?"

Shane huffed out a breath. "She won't be happy when I find her. Let's put it that way."

"Then why would she leave you such a hint?"

"I told you: She's clever. She thinks we're all dancing to her tune." He tapped the hilt of his sheathed saber. "I'm betting I have a move or two that will surprise her."

Anya paused as if she wanted to say more, but only bit her lip and nodded as she resumed hacking away. "It is not far," she said after a moment. "I will take you to the temple, but no farther."

They continued for a while in silence. Shane took a turn with the machete, and his arm quickly began to ache. It was a far different tool than his saber, which was lighter and felt more like an extension of his arm. He kept his eyes peeled for animals, but though he heard many birds and beasts, all he saw was the occasional bug.

"What do I do if I see a frog?" he asked. "Will they actually attack a person?"

Anya's tinkling laugh rang out again. "No, no. Here, let me have this." She took the machete from him and reclaimed her spot in the lead. "A snake is venomous. Yes? It will bite you and inject its poison directly into your blood."

Shane shuddered. "Right."

"These jungle frogs are not venomous, but poisonous. They have no way to break your skin and put their toxin inside you." Anya cast a glance back at him. "Do not put one in your mouth, and you will be fine."

Shane chuckled at that. "I suppose I'll be fine, then."

"Do you know how they become poisonous?" she asked. "They are not born this way. As little tadpoles, their mother lays eggs for them to eat. But because the mother is poisonous, the eggs are poisonous, too. The tadpoles eat just a little poison at a time, and it builds up slowly, so that it does not hurt them. But by the time they are frogs, they are deadly to any bird or snake that would eat them. The bright colors are a warning to predators: I am dangerous, and I taste bad. Stay away."

"Sort of like a Greencloak," Shane said under his breath.

"Pardon?" she asked.

"Nothing. It's a private—"

Just then a great roar rang out from nearby. It turned the sweat running down Shane's back to ice. More worrying to him, it seemed to have the same effect on Anya.

"What was that?" she said, standing suddenly still.

"You don't know?" he hissed. "You're the guide!"

She backed away from the direction from which the sound had come and held her machete up. "That is not a cat nor a monkey. That's a sound that doesn't belong in the jungle."

Shane drew his own blade. "How far to the temple?"

Anya inclined her head to one side. "It is that way. Only a few minutes' walk."

"I suggest we run," Shane said. Anya nodded, then took off through the trees, ducking her head low and keeping the machete at her side.

Something big was following, crashing through the underbrush. Shane hoped the branches and vines would slow the thing down, but when he risked a glance over his shoulder, he saw it closing in on them.

It was a bear. A massive bear, so big he could have believed it was Suka herself. But Suka was dead, and this bear's matted coat was the color of chocolate, which only made its yellowish-white bladelike teeth more noticeable.

"It's a bear!" he cried to Anya.

"Impossible!" she answered without looking back. "We don't have bears here."

"Tell that to the bear!"

Shane felt heat at the back of his neck, and he didn't know if it was from his own exertion or if the animal was breathing on him, close enough now to swipe him to the ground with its massive clawed paw. He pushed himself harder, desperate to get away, fearful that any step might be his last.

And then he heard an unfamiliar voice shouting, "This way!"

An arrow passed overhead, then another, and Shane saw they had been fired from a clearing ahead, from which he could hear shouts of encouragement. Anya launched herself from the tree line, and he followed on her heels, crashing into the clearing, which was dominated by a massive pyramidal structure of yellowish stone, overrun with vines. There were men in the clearing, too. Two archers trained their bows on the jungle at his back, and a third man stood at an open doorway at the base of the pyramid, waving them forward urgently.

"Go, go, go, go!" he shouted. Shane heard in his voice that the man was a soldier.

Anya didn't hesitate, and he didn't either. They ran full tilt into the doorway, and the three soldiers followed, one of them keeping his bow taut and aimed outside while the other two heaved the large stone door closed behind them.

It took a full minute for them to regain their breath. Shane dropped his head between his knees and gulped hungrily at the air. The archers had disappeared, but the man who'd held the door for them stood by patiently, leaning against the stone wall of the short hallway they'd entered. The hallway itself was unlit, but light came from the temple's interior.

When he'd regained his composure, Shane turned to the man, who wore the black leathers of a Conqueror. "Thank you," he said. "We were in real trouble there."

Recognition flashed in the man's eyes, but he quickly masked it. The Conquerors had been told that Shane's identity as the Reptile King must be kept a secret. Outside of Stetriol, they were supposed to pretend he was no more than their commander's nephew.

"You're the captain?" Shane asked.

"Captain Lovvorn. Yes." He seemed stuck halfway between a bow and a salute, unsure how to address his flushed and bedraggled king. "Can I . . . get you anything?"

"Information," Shane answered. "What is going on here? Are you under attack?"

"Under attack?" Anya huffed, her breath slow to return to her.

"That bear has to be a spirit animal," Shane explained.

"Yes," said the captain. "And, er, no. Please, follow me inside and I'll explain." The captain led them down the short hallway, which ended in a large central space, a stone room at the heart of the pyramid. Its walls sloped inward as they reached up, but rather than coming to a point, they ended high above in a square-shaped opening, like a window over their heads. The opening was small, but midday sunlight poured into the space, where six other soldiers loitered about, stopping mid-conversation to watch the newcomers. One of them had a thick, bloody bandage on his thigh. Another had scabbed slash marks across his face, and a third looked like he was wasting away, a haunted look in his heavy-lidded eyes. They were all dirty, and where their flesh was visible through the muck, it was slick with sweat.

"What in Erdas happened here?" Shane asked.

"Our spirit animals have gone mad," the captain said. "That beast you encountered was Soyland's." He inclined his head toward one of the archers. "Most of them were content to slither or scamper away when the ... after everything, but not that monster of a bear. She's a mean old thing. I didn't think animals held grudges."

"We've been trapped here for weeks," Soyland added. "She won't listen to me. I've tried. I don't understand what went wrong."

Shane cursed silently. He'd heard of this happening, of course. In the weeks since Gerathon and Kovo's defeat, Conquerors all over the world had been losing their spirit animals. With the Bile gone, its power to compel was dwindling. It was only a matter of time before everyone who had used it to force a bond would find that their once-doting animal companions had opinions of their own.

Shane absently touched the spot on his chest where his

own spirit animal slept as a tattoo. He hadn't released Grahv since hearing the news that Bile bonds were fading. How long would it be before the crocodile was freed? Would he seek Shane just as ferociously?

"What are you doing here to begin with?" asked Anya.

Captain Lovvorn's eyes cut toward Shane.

Shane sighed. "They're the advance force of an invading army," he said. "Holed up here while they await orders."

"How do you know that?" she asked.

"Because it's *my* orders they're awaiting."

Captain Lovvorn, obviously uncomfortable with the ruse and glad to have it be over, dropped quickly to one knee, and his men began to follow his lead.

"Enough of that," Shane said. "Up. I'm not in charge of anybody anymore."

The men looked to their captain, perplexed, while an altogether different emotion flashed in Anya's eyes. "They're Conquerors." She drew her machete from her bag. "You're the Devourer."

The men drew their own weapons, aiming them at Anya.

"Everybody calm down," Shane said, holding up his hands. "Nobody do anything stupid."

"Stupid, like walk into a Conqueror den?"

"The Conquerors don't exist anymore," Shane said. "These are just men. And they're your best bet at getting out of here alive."

"I don't know about that," said Anya. "I'm thinking we throw Soyland to the bear and she lets us go."

Soyland gulped audibly at Shane's back.

"We're not throwing anyone to the bear."

"Then we shoot it. I have poison arrows."

"No!" Shane shouted, and his voice echoed in the oddly shaped chamber. "No," he said more calmly. "The bear was a victim in all this. Poisoning her isn't right."

After a moment of silence, the captain shrugged. "Wouldn't be easy, anyway. We've had archers up top for weeks. She doesn't show herself till one of us is outside the walls, and even then she stays safely within the foliage."

Shane sucked air through his teeth. "Unbelievable. I walked right into her trap."

"The bear's?" Anya asked.

"No, the woman's. Yumaris led me here." He rubbed his temples. " 'Bushmaster' was what we called this operation. We—We named them all after snakes."

"She led you here," Anya repeated. "So that a confused and angry bear could maul you or trap you indoors until the food ran out?" She considered the tip of her machete, then dropped it to her side. "Isn't that a bit elaborate? There are much easier ways to get rid of someone."

Shane blinked. "You're right. Of course you're right. Then why . . . ?"

The bear's eerie roar rang out from the jungle beyond the temple's walls.

"Captain, I'm going to want to debrief you and your men. One at a time. I want to know everything that's happened here. Everything you've seen. Anya." He turned to her. "I want you with the other archers up on the wall tonight. My guess is they're exhausted, and a fresh set of eyes will do wonders."

Anya huffed. "So much for not being in charge of anybody."

"It's just a suggestion."

She looked at him appraisingly. "It's a good one. So I'll do what you say. For now. But when this is over, I'm going home. And you and your pet soldiers better go right back to Stetriol."

"Sounds good to me," said Shane, but he had a strong feeling it wouldn't be nearly so simple.

As night fell, they built a cooking fire on one side of the stone chamber. The evening was warm, but the fire brought light and the smell of cooking beans, and it was welcome.

Shane sat down away from the firelight, but not so far that he couldn't cross the distance quickly if danger found them. Had they been under siege by a bird of prey instead of a bear, they would be in trouble, as their fortress stood open and indefensible against the night sky. The stars shone bright and unobstructed.

He spoke first to Captain Lovvorn, and learned that all had gone well for their first month stationed at the temple. As Shane knew, they were the advance guard in the Conquerors' planned invasion of Clarobo. The city served a valuable function as a port; if it fell, the entire continent would be instantly vulnerable. And Clarobo would fall quickly if forced to defend itself on two fronts, with one attack coming from the Conquerors' fleet at sea as a second attack was launched from the jungle.

So Lovvorn and his men had been told to secure a post and wait. They were still waiting when disaster struck.

It had been a normal morning. Exercises at dawn; card games over their morning oatmeal. Then there was a sound that wasn't a sound, a hissing in their heads that felt like cold fingers in their brains. There was a flash of anger, a rush of panic, and then silence.

"We all looked at one another," the captain explained. "Wondering whether every one of us had experienced the same thing. My first thought was that it was some kind of assault – that the Greencloaks had found us." His eyes had a faraway look, as if he were watching the events of that morning unfold all over again. "Before I could say it, we were attacked – but not by Greencloaks. It was our animals. Our own spirit animals. They'd gone . . . well, wild, though it seems strange to say it. I didn't know it was possible."

Shane nodded solemnly.

"It wasn't just us. Was it?" the captain asked.

"No. It was everyone. Everyone who drank the Bile."

"What happened?"

"It's complicated," Shane answered, running his hands through his hair. "Suffice it to say, we lost. The Greencloaks outmaneuvered us. Our allies are . . . gone. With the Bile neutralized, we lost half our army in an instant. Our forces started withdrawing immediately, trying to get to Stetriol as quickly as possible, before the enemy realized just how powerless we were."

"But you came here. For us." Lovvorn smiled. "I'm honored, sir."

Shane rubbed his hands together. The truth was that he'd known the Bushmaster plan was in the works, but he'd had no idea men had actually been sent to Amaya. He'd left the military decisions to others while he'd focused on obtaining the talismans. Most likely Gar had stationed these men here, acting on Gerathon's orders. It would never have occurred to Shane to look for them. But there was no point in turning down the man's gratitude, and he accepted it with a curt nod.

"I want to speak to your men," Shane said. "I'd like to get to know everyone."

"I'll send Soyland your way, sir."

"No," said Shane. "I want to start with him." And he pointed to the scrawny soldier with the haunted eyes, who watched them intently from the far side of the fire and quickly turned away as Shane singled him out.

Shane remained seated when the soldier approached and bent down on one knee.

"Up," Shane said. "Up, up. I've seen enough bowing to last me a long time. Have a proper seat."

"Yes, my liege," the soldier said, and his voice squeaked. He wasn't much older than Shane, and he was skinny, barely filling out his leathers. Shane tried to picture him in the steel gauntlets and shoulder plates the Conquerors wore over their oiled black leather armor when they went on the march, but he had a hard time imagining this boy ever being an imposing sight.

Shane wondered briefly how many young men and women of Stetriol had marched into battle across Erdas. He'd once feared their numbers weren't enough. Now it seemed far too many—too many lives, for a gambit that had failed.

The boy sat as directed, but he remained rigid, staring straight ahead as if at attention.

"What's your name?"

"Alix, sir."

"Alix. Tell me about when the animals turned against you," Shane prompted.

"It was . . . It was chaos. As if the animals had been sleeping, and then suddenly they were awake. You never want to corner an animal, you know? It was like they'd all been cornered and had only just realized, all at once. Garth's owl tried to take his eyes out. It just kept screeching and smacking him with its wings. It hadn't seemed so big before. The captain's horse was kicking at anybody who came close. Arnold's snake slithered off – somewhere. I'm terrified it's still in here with us. Tep's lynx actually got into it with Dahved's dog, which was lucky for us, because we had our hands full with the bear."

"Soyland's bear," Shane clarified.

"Yes, sir. We led it out – well, to be honest, we just sort of ran away, and it followed. Then we were able to double back and lock ourselves in here. The owl had flown away by then, and the other animals scattered. We kept expecting the bear to wander off eventually, too. But every time we leave the temple, she's there. Waiting."

Shane narrowed his eyes. "And where was your spirit animal in all of this?"

"Mine? Uh, in the confusion – I'm not sure . . ."

"Your captain told me what you'd bonded with. And I find it hard to believe any amount of confusion would allow it to slip away."

Alix swallowed hard. "Sir, please don't—"

"Tell me what you're hiding. That's an order."

Alix wiped the sweat from his brow. He swallowed once more and, eyes downcast, nodded curtly. Then his left hand went to his right bracer. Slowly, he undid the clasps at his wrist and below his elbow, and the leather bracer fell away. He held his forearm up to Shane, catching the light of the fire.

There on his arm was an image of a ram. The tattoo was faded at the edges, as if somehow going out of focus, and the skin beneath and all around it was a sickly white, dry and peeling.

"I can't summon him anymore. I've tried. He just . . . I think he's stuck or something. Stuck like that.

"And the mark . . . It's starting to itch."

"What use is an earthworm?"

In the days following his father's death, when Shane had ascended to the throne and taken the mantle of the Reptile King, change came quickly. He did everything he could to spread the word: There was a cure for the bonding sickness, and Shane had it.

People came to the capital in droves, more each day, so that Shane could barely keep up with the demand. Yet he and Zerif trusted no one with the secret of the Bile's creation. Each and every drop was a drop made by their hands.

The secret gave Shane power—more power even than the crown he had inherited. It gave him the power to put

Gar in his place. It gave him the power to unite Stetriol under his leadership, not out of fear or tradition, but love and respect. Gratitude.

Best of all, it gave Shane the power to defy the Greencloaks. He could have revenge against them for all they'd done to Stetriol – all they *hadn't* done *for* Stetriol.

So once the bonding sickness had been wiped out, Shane and Zerif didn't stop creating Bile. They wouldn't stop until every able-bodied, battle-ready man and woman on the continent had a spirit animal.

People chose animals based on how they would contribute to the war effort. Predators were most popular. Some chose animals for their fearsome teeth, their speed, their ability to fly or crush or sneak.

And then there was Yumaris, who made an unusual choice.

"What use is an earthworm?" Shane asked her, unable to keep the irritation from his voice. It was the day before they would leave Stetriol, perhaps forever. Zerif was already abroad, gathering allies and laying the groundwork for their invasion. Shane had decided to pay one last visit to the small cemetery in the shadow of the castle, the one where his parents were buried. He hadn't expected to find Yumaris here.

"All creatures of Erdas have use," she answered.

Shane rolled his eyes. He'd had little patience for her cryptic answers as her student. He certainly didn't care for them as her king. "Some less use than others," he said pointedly.

"Earthworms are extraordinary animals, in fact," she said. Joints practically creaking with age, she knelt down over the grave of long-dead King Feliandor and placed her small, writhing spirit animal upon the ground. The grayish-pink worm flailed for a moment, then, in a few pulsating movements that made Shane's skin crawl, it burrowed into the soil.

It struck him as somewhat disrespectful, but then, Feliandor wasn't actually buried here. The grave was only symbolic.

When the Greencloaks had finished with Good King Fel, there hadn't been enough left of him to bury.

"They have no eyes. No ears." Yumaris stood, pulling herself up with her walking stick, her movements as slow and deliberate as her words. "They do not *see* or *hear* so much as *sense*." She shrugged. "For them, that is enough. They survive. They thrive. All beneath the feet of giants."

Shane snorted. "And they eat dirt."

"Aye, dirt," said Yumaris. She held out her bony wrist, and the earthworm reappeared upon her papery skin as a tattoo. "The dirt of Stetriol's great kings. One last taste of home before we go to conquer."

She turned away then and shuffled back to the castle, leaving Shane alone among the tombstones.

Alone among the fallen kings and queens of Stetriol.

Food for worms, all of them.

Shane slept fitfully that night upon the hard dirt floor. He woke at first light, as did the soldiers, who went about their morning routines gloomily.

Of all of them, Alix seemed to greet the day with new enthusiasm. Shane hadn't known what to tell him about his warped tattoo, other than to promise he would try to help. That had apparently been enough for Alix. The haunted look was gone from his eyes, and though he kept his bracer on over his mark, he moved about as if a weight had been lifted from him.

"We're running low on just about everything but water," he explained apologetically as he handed Shane and Anya bowls of boiled oats. "It rains enough—that's not a problem. But we're almost out of food."

"Tell the cook not to worry about rationing," Shane said, poking at his unappetizing mush. "Use it all up. We're getting out of here today."

Alix smiled and nodded. "Yes, sir," he said, and trotted off to relay the message.

Shane pulled Anya aside. "What do you know about this place?"

"Not much," she said, crossing her arms. "Other than that it's been seized by an enemy force." Clearly she hadn't yet forgiven him for once trying to conquer the world.

"I'm sorry I got you into this," he said. "You only wanted to help."

She frowned. "You're not what I expected, you know."

"Let me guess." Shane grinned. "You thought I'd be taller?"

"Actually, yes. Taller and . . . sharper. Scarier. And cackling like a madman."

"There's not been much to laugh about. Listen, everything is a little more complicated than most people think.

Most of your information about the war was filtered through the Greencloaks, and the Greencloaks only like to tell the stories where they play the role of the hero."

Anya's gaze swept over the men gathered around the fire, picking at their breakfast. "I suppose we're in this together, as they say." Her eyes came back to pin Shane. "Assuming your priority is escape. Yes? You wish to survive this, and save your men?"

"Of course I do."

"And if you had to choose between the lives of these men and revenge on this woman you seek, which would you choose?"

"No one else dies," Shane said hotly. "Not on account of Yumaris's actions. And she's definitely behind this, somehow. She wanted me to find this place. So I'll ask again: What's special about it?"

Anya shrugged. "It is one of many temples in the area. They were built long ago by our ancestors, but their original purpose has been lost to time."

"Are the others open at the top like this?"

"I don't know," said Anya. "I was wondering whether this site was built to honor Essix. That would explain why it's open to the sky."

"Maybe," Shane said, looking up into the clouds. But somehow the idea didn't ring true. "I'm going to have a look around."

Shane refused to believe this was a dead end. Yumaris had always had a way of seeing two steps ahead, and he could very easily believe she had led him here for a reason he didn't see, perhaps to deal with the freed spirit animals. Should he let Grahv out and hope for the best? Maybe he could even get the crocodile and the bear to occupy each other while Shane and the others fled.

But so far, every step Yumaris had made since fleeing the Conqueror camp had led Shane directly to her next stop. She was leaving bread crumbs for him, and he had a nagging suspicion he hadn't found the end of the trail.

Several stone passageways led away from the central chamber, curling in on themselves. Many came to dead ends or empty rooms, the purposes of which Shane couldn't guess. Two rose up to balconies set high on the outside of the structure. He found the archers on watch there, and they pointed out to him the odd design that ran around the pyramid, visible only from that angle. There was a ridge carved along the outer walls, running at a gradual decline all the way down.

"It's like a ramp carved out of the sides of the walls," he said.

"But too narrow for a man to walk on," said one archer.

"Or a bear," said the other. "Happily. From above, it would almost look like a spiral."

Shane startled at that. "I'll be back," he said, then retraced his steps through the winding hallways until he came to a dead end he remembered from before. Unlike all the other walls in the place, this one was marked with a spiral design.

"Maybe it's nothing," Shane said. He pushed against the wall, but it didn't give. So he ran back to the inner chamber and enlisted some help.

"If it's a door, I can't budge it," said Lovvorn as he strained against it.

"Let's try all together," Shane suggested. He pressed his shoulder in beside Lovvorn's, and Anya shoved, too, but it wasn't until Alix joined in that the stone slab began to creak slowly open.

"You're stronger than you look, Alix!" Anya beamed as they continued to push.

The soldier blushed. "It's a team effort," he said.

The door opened onto a tunnel. Where all before had been stone, the pathway behind the hidden door was carved entirely from dirt.

"Do you think it's safe?" Anya asked.

"Absolutely not," Shane said. "You said it yourself, Anya: Everything in this jungle is out to get us."

She sighed. "Let me get a torch."

"It's like a giant earthworm tunnel," Shane said, and he shuddered when the words had left his mouth. Where Yumaris was concerned, he didn't really believe in coincidence.

The tunnel sloped downward, slowly at first, and more steeply as they went. If not for the light of Anya's torch, they would have been shrouded in utter darkness. Eventually they came to a branch in the path.

"This way slopes upward," Lovvorn said, gesturing to their left. "And I'm not sure. . . . I think there's daylight ahead. It's faint, but I can just make it out."

"This way goes farther down," Alix said, pointing to the right-hand path. His nose wrinkled. "It stinks. It smells like . . . death."

"Well," Anya said lightly, "that's an easy choice, isn't it?"

"I have to go down," Shane said.

"Sir," said Lovvorn.

"Sire!" said Alix.

"Idiot," said Anya. "What are you thinking?"

"She led me here. I'm certain she wants me to see whatever is down there. You three go on. Make sure that's a way out. Then go back for the others. We've gone far enough that it should lead us right past the bear."

"Let me go with you," Alix said.

"I have to do this alone, Alix," Shane said. "But I'll catch up."

Anya lit a second torch from her own and gave it to Shane. He chuckled at the look she gave him as she handed it over.

"Cackling like a madman," she said. "I knew it."

And with that, Shane descended into the unknown.

Shane walked for long minutes as the passageway sloped and slanted, curving around like a slow and subtle spiral.

The silence was absolute except for the snap and hiss of the torch in his hands and the slow shuffle of his boots on the packed dirt. On a hunch, he stopped, standing totally still . . . and the sounds of boots on dirt continued from behind him. He was being followed.

Shane turned and waited, sword drawn. He wasn't surprised when Anya stepped into the sphere of light cast by his torch. She was gripping her machete, and her eyes flicked down to his saber.

"I need to stop sneaking up on you, don't I?" she asked.

"You really do."

Anya bit her lip. "I thought you could use some company. I was just—"

Shane struck without warning. He sprung forward, slamming his sword's pommel into Anya's cheek just as he looped a foot behind her legs. She toppled, falling onto her back in the dirt, and Shane had his blade to her chin before she even seemed to register that she'd been struck.

"You bite your lip whenever you tell a lie, Anya," he said.

Anya blinked, confusion in her eyes. "Shane, what . . . Have you lost your mind?"

"Just my patience," he said. "Where is she?"

Anya didn't move a muscle, but the fierceness returned to her gaze. "I'm trying to help you."

"I noticed," Shane said. "You still haven't named your price for escorting me into the deadly Amayan jungle. Awfully generous of you, working for free. And then we ended up here, of all places."

"You asked to go to a temple," she countered.

"And you said there were several in the area. But we just happened to end up at the one overrun with Conquerors. That's a big coincidence."

Anya's scowl deepened.

"But the bow and arrows? That was an inspired little piece of manipulation. Did she tell you I have a weak spot for girl archers? Did she think I'd be more likely to trust you if you reminded me of someone I care about? Don't think I didn't notice that every time you needed a weapon, you went for the machete. Have you ever even used a bow?"

She looked ready to spit fire at him, but still she didn't speak.

"Where is Yumaris?" Shane hissed, fighting to keep his rage under control.

"I don't know." Anya ground out the words, simmering with fury herself. "She paid me to lead you here. To this temple. She didn't say anything about Conquerors or . . . or crazed spirit animals. And she certainly didn't mention you were out to kill her."

Shane lowered his weapon. "You did what she paid you for. Get out of here."

Anya scrambled to her feet but showed no interest in leaving. "Whatever twisted game the two of you are playing here—you can walk away from it, Shane!"

He shook his head. "I can't, though. I can't forgive her for what she did. Not ever."

"But you would like Erdas to forgive you, though. Right?"

"That's different," Shane said sullenly. "I was—I was tricked. I only ever wanted to make the world a better place." He hung his head. "I'd only just gotten Drina back and—"

"And she was a monster," came a raspy voice from the darkness.

Shane swung around, raising the torch as high as he could in the cramped space.

She crept forward slowly. Shane could hear the clomp of her staff, the shuffle of her feet. Clomp, shuffle, clomp. She stopped some yards away, where the light only barely reached her, but Shane could see that it was Yumaris. She was filthy and shrunken, even smaller than he'd remembered, almost lost in the folds of her cloak. Her face was shrouded in shadow.

"My king," she rasped in greeting.

Shane gritted his teeth and held up his saber.

"King of dead things," she continued. "Dead lands, dead ambitions."

"Dead tutors," Shane said. "You know why I'm here, Yumaris."

"I do," she said. "You blame me for your sister's death."

"Of course I *blame you*," he growled, taking a step forward. "You killed her. You killed Drina!"

"The serpent killed your sister."

Shane sneered. "You held her down."

"And you gave her the Bile," Yumaris responded calmly. "And Zerif led you to that, because Kovo bid him to. And on and on."

He took another step. "You're not escaping the blame for what you did."

"And will you, Devourer? Escape the blame for all you've done?" She clucked her tongue. "Once we drank the Bile, weren't we all Gerathon's puppets? Perhaps none of us were responsible for our actions in the war. Perhaps we all deserve to be pardoned."

Anya touched Shane's shoulder lightly. "Maybe she's right, Shane. Maybe there's a peaceful solution here."

Shane shuddered with barely suppressed rage. He shrugged her hand away. "She claims to see the future, you know," he told her, eyes still on Yumaris's shadowed form. "Is that what you see now, Yumaris, when you peer into the mists of time? Conquerors and Greencloaks living in peace and harmony? Singing happy songs?"

"I do not *see* or *hear* so much as *sense*," Yumaris said sharply. "I can make predictions." She tilted her cloaked head toward Anya. "I can pay girls to help those predictions along, just in case. I'm never quite sure until the final moment whether a person will go left or right. Up or down. But I can sense which way they lean." Yumaris took a shuffling step forward, and the light of the torch illuminated her pointed chin and her dry, cracked lips. "Gerathon was going to kill one of you that day. By stepping in when I did, I ensured it wasn't you."

Shane shook his head sadly. "You made the wrong choice."

"Drina was not well, and you know it. The bonding sickness had left her twisted. Wicked. Vicious. And is it any wonder?" She clucked her tongue again, sadly this time. "We adults feed our children a steady diet of poison, and then we're surprised to find they've grown up to be poisonous."

Shane narrowed his eyes. There was something odd about the way she tilted her head. Something suspicious about the way she stood just past the threshold of shadow. "What are you using for light down here, Yumaris?" he asked. "Where is your torch?"

"And then there's you," she continued, ignoring his question entirely. "Crossing the world in pursuit of vengeance — an evil act. But you've done good along the way. Helped people. *Inspired* people." She let out a dry chuckle. "I wish I could see for myself how you've grown."

Yumaris stepped fully into the light then, and pulled

back her hood. Anya gasped, and Shane felt a wave of revulsion. Revulsion . . . and pity.

It was her eyes. Her eyes were gone. In the hollows where they'd been there was now only pink flesh.

"What happened to you?" Shane croaked.

"The world is on the precipice of great change," she said. "I saw the signs myself, and they are the last things I will ever see."

"What does that mean?" Anya asked, her composure cracking.

"The Wyrm is coming," Yumaris hissed. "And Erdas is in terrible danger." She tilted her head again, and the light shone flat against that eerie skin. "The world above will need a protector who can walk the line between good and evil. Light and shadow."

"The world . . . above?" echoed Shane.

"You've visited every continent on Erdas this year, my king. And yet you've only seen half the world." She flashed her crooked teeth. "Spare my life, and there is still much that I could teach a willing pupil. Kill me . . . and Erdas may pay a steep price."

Shane gripped the hilt of his sword so hard it hurt. His face was placid, but his gut was a swirl of conflicting emotions. Part of him wanted to strike her down, just to prove that he could. To show that she had no power over him. That no one would ever have power over him again.

But he'd never been as bloodthirsty as Drina — that much was true.

What if the rest of what Yumaris had said was true as well?

What if he had a chance to redeem himself?

"Shane, no," Anya said, and she tugged at him, turning his eyes away from Yumaris. "Remember what I said," she whispered. "You can walk away from this. Right up this slope." She smiled, but her eyes were sad. "The sun is shining up there. The war is over. Let someone else play at being the hero."

"I'm not a hero," Shane said. "I know that. But I'm not a villain either. I'm a king." He turned away from Anya, and his eyes fell again upon the hunched horror Yumaris had become. "And a king uses all the tools at his disposal."

Yumaris shuffled off into the darkness, and Shane followed her. He didn't hesitate, and he didn't look back.

But as the darkness closed around him, the tattoo on his chest began to itch.

PART 4

VENTURE

*"The Greencloaks have
many fine qualities, but
there are stories that they'd
prefer to forget."*

*— Fall of the Beasts:
Book 1:* Immortal Guardians

THE NIGHT BREEZE WAS COOL AND CARRIED THE SCENT of the ocean, but Shane was in no position to enjoy it. Inside the rough burlap sack that had been shoved over his head, the air was warm and sour. He couldn't smell anything but his own breath.

He stumbled, his foot catching on a rock or root, and he would have crashed to the ground if not for the hands gripping his elbows. Two soldiers were leading him up the steeply inclined path. His captors kept him from falling, but they weren't gentle. They held his arms tight enough to bruise.

Shane knew they were nearing their destination when the ground leveled out. They had reached the peak of the island, which rose like a single flat-topped mountain from the ocean. The sounds of people echoed through the night – a lot of people.

It sounded like an army.

"Who goes there?" called a voice.

"It's us," said the soldier to Shane's left.

There was a sound of rattling chains, then the groan of metal hinges as a gate swung open. His captors shoved him forward without another word, and Shane stepped past walls he could not see.

He counted one hundred and twelve steps before a kick to the back of his legs brought him down hard on his knees.

"Stay," growled one of the soldiers.

The other said, "Tell Maddox to get out here."

Shane tested the rope that bound his hands. The knot held tight.

Without warning, the sack was torn from his head, and Shane squinted in the torchlight. A figure loomed above him: a scowling beast of a man, thick of neck and shoulder, with a matted red beard and a crooked nose once broken and poorly healed. His eyebrows rose nearly to his bald pate as recognition lit his craggy features.

"Well, now," the man – Maddox – rumbled. "I must be coming up in the world if royalty is bowing to me."

"It's a new experience for me too," Shane said.

"Is it? Because I'd heard otherwise." Maddox smiled, showing crooked, broken teeth. "I'd heard that our king had taken to kneeling to just about anybody. Great Beasts. Foreigners with fancy beards." He drew his tongue across those jagged teeth. *"Greencloaks."*

Shane spat at the man's feet. "I've never knelt to a Greencloak. Give me my weapon back and say that again."

Maddox threw back his head and laughed. The torchlight gleamed off of his armor, and Shane caught sight of the symbol emblazoned on his chest plate: an angular *C* ringed with spikes.

"I'm not here to cause trouble, Maddox."

"That's *General* Maddox to you . . . Shane," the man said, obviously refusing to use Shane's own title. The message was clear. Here, in this armed camp on this volcanic island in the middle of Oceanus, Shane was not a king.

It didn't bother Shane. He had bigger things to worry about.

Bigger, older, more terrifying things.

"Just what *are* you doing here on my island?" Maddox demanded.

"Haven't you guessed? I'm here to join you."

Maddox lifted an eyebrow.

"All hail the New Conquerors," Shane said with a wicked smile.

A young man named Abhay was tasked with escorting Shane to an open cot. He eyed Shane warily, but unlike Maddox and the soldiers who had dragged him up from the beach, Abhay wasn't from Stetriol—and he didn't have an obvious grudge.

"You were Maddox's king?" he asked as he led Shane across the campgrounds. The entire site sat inside a caldera, a natural depression in the landscape. Once, when Erdas was young, this island had been an active volcano. Now it was a lush green mountain, one of the Hundred Isles. From this high up, the island would offer a spectacular view of the ocean on all sides . . . if not for the high wooden wall that encircled the campsite.

There was a single watchtower in the east, and a single chained gate below it.

Only one way in, Shane noted. And one way out.

"I *am* Maddox's king," he corrected. "He's just angry and throwing his weight around. Sometimes grown men throw the biggest tantrums."

"There were rumors . . ." Abhay hesitated. "People said that, at the end, you fought alongside the Greencloaks."

"It's a lot more complicated than that. But I never stopped fighting for Stetriol." Shane paused as they skirted the edge of a training ground, a large open space among the rows and rows of tents. Men and women had partnered up for sparring. Most wore the oiled leathers and metal pauldrons of the Conquerors, but nobody seemed to have a full set. Missing pieces of the uniform had been replaced, giving the entire militia a patchwork quality. They sparred with swords and maces, staves and battered shields—apparently anything they'd been able to find.

"A little rough around the edges," Shane said.

Abhay shrugged. "Maybe. But it's home."

"You really think of this place that way?"

He shrugged again. "For now."

"I recognize your accent," Shane said. "Southeastern Zhong, right? Beautiful place."

"I thought so too," Abhay said sadly. "That's why I decided to help the Conquerors."

Shane wrinkled his brow in confusion. "I don't follow."

Abhay turned to watch a sparring match between two young women armed with swords and shields. "I love my homeland, and I fought fiercely to protect it—at first. But the more we fought against the Conquerors, the more ruin they brought. Zhong burned all around us. I only wanted to put out the flames." He sighed. "I was a message runner for the resistance. It was an easy thing to betray them to your army. But your army lost anyway, and I was branded a traitor."

Abhay lapsed into silence, and the clang of swords on shields rushed in to fill the space.

"I had no place to go," he said at last. "Your war cost me my home. I don't blame you – I made my choice. But when I heard that Maddox had put out the call . . . that he was offering a place to those who needed it . . . well, I leaped at the chance."

"Even if it means going to war all over again?" Shane asked.

"You don't understand," Abhay said. "For us, the war never ended."

Shane dreamed he summoned a wolf.

They ran alongside their pack, hunting by the light of the moon.

And he knew he'd never be alone again.

Morning dawned bright and beautiful. With nothing to obscure the view, the sky above the caldera seemed huge, a vast dome of blue broken only by swift-moving clouds and wheeling, diving seabirds.

By the light of day, Maddox's operation was more impressive than it had seemed the night before. There were no fewer than two hundred men and women within the campsite's walls, all of whom seemed to have one task or another that morning, from guard duty to food preparation to waste disposal. There was a blacksmith reforging damaged weapons, a leatherworker stitching a scuffed and battered bracer, and a farrier outfitting one of several horses with new shoes.

But Shane was inevitably drawn back to the training grounds at the very center of the caldera. There was no way around it – the militia was a long way from being ready for true combat. Everywhere he looked, he saw evidence of fighters who had come to rely on spirit animal bonds – bonds that had evaporated when the Bile had lost its power. It was like watching men and women who had lost a limb relearning combat from scratch.

Rumor had it that Maddox had an elite band of warriors at his disposal. But if that was true, they weren't on the training grounds this morning.

He saw Abhay facing off against a pale-skinned girl with short black hair. They were both awkward; their technique was sloppy, even lazy. As their wooden swords clacked against each other, Shane realized neither of them was trying very hard.

His uncle, Gar, had insisted on daily weapons training back in Stetriol. Shane had resisted for a long time, having little interest in the arts of war. Now he recognized that same reluctance in every swing of Abhay's sword.

As he watched, Shane thought he caught a scent of something on the breeze – a foul smell, strangely familiar. But the wind shifted and the scent was gone, replaced with the salty tang of the ocean all around them.

Suddenly a heavy hand came down upon his shoulder. Maddox towered above him.

"Let's see what you can do," the man grumbled, and he gestured at the rack of weapons to one side.

Shane flashed a smile. "I thought you'd never ask, General." He strolled along the weapons rack, ignoring the din of the people fighting all around him and evaluating his options. He saw his own sword, the curved saber that had been confiscated when he'd surrendered at the watchman's outpost at the foot of the mountain. It hung there among swords of all types—long swords and short swords, needlelike rapiers and two-handed claymores, and the ornate katana blades favored in some parts of Zhong.

He could beat Maddox with a sword. No question.

But it was hard to hold back with a sword. And stabbing the New Conquerors' general on his first day probably wouldn't help him blend in.

He selected a quarterstaff. It was well balanced, with greater reach than any sword but far less deadly.

Then he turned and saw Maddox had chosen a morning star. It was as brutal a weapon as Shane had ever seen: a massive, spiked iron ball at the end of a heavy chain.

Maddox's hideous smile split his face. "I have a feeling only one of us is going to enjoy this."

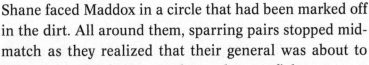

Shane faced Maddox in a circle that had been marked off in the dirt. All around them, sparring pairs stopped midmatch as they realized that their general was about to fight—and *who* their general was about to fight.

He heard them murmuring. Some called him the king. Others called him a traitor. He had to block it all out. He had to focus . . . on the huge spiked sphere already arcing toward him.

Shane easily sidestepped the blow, jabbing Maddox in the ribs as the morning star struck dirt.

Maddox shifted his bulk, bringing his arms back and swinging the spiked ball up and around. Shane dodged again, jabbed again, stepped back. Maddox's style was reckless; with the weight of his weapon, his moves were easy to anticipate, and he left himself open to attack. But the general was clearly betting that he could land one blow before all of Shane's smaller hits could add up to anything. That single blow, coming from such a power-house, would likely be enough to end the fight.

The morning star struck dirt again, and Shane knew Maddox would need precious seconds to pull it free. He stepped forward, not anticipating that Maddox would release his grip on his weapon with one hand and lash out. The general backhanded him full in the face and Shane saw stars, but he swung around with the momentum of the blow, whirling to smack Maddox across the temple with his staff.

A sharp crack rang out, and Maddox grunted. He'd felt that.

Shane couldn't help it—he smiled.

Yumaris had warned him about just this sort of thing. He still didn't understand just how much of the future she could see, if any. But she had an undeniable and uncanny ability to predict what people would do . . . and the trouble they would get into.

She had a special knack for pointing out Shane's short-comings, and pride ranked high on the list. She'd told him before he'd set sail: *Sometimes you have to lose a battle to win a war.*

Beating up Maddox wouldn't put him in charge of the militia, and it might even get him thrown out of the camp.

But, oh, how he wanted to trash this guy.

He burst into motion, leaping over the spiked ball and smacking Maddox three times before his feet touched the ground again. He ducked under Maddox's next swing and slapped his staff against the man's knees. For every one of Maddox's attacks, Shane struck the general two or three times. Maddox was tough, but he could only take so much.

The crowd was closing in around their circle, strangely quiet. There was no cheering or jeering or slapping of backs. But they observed with focused intensity, almost as if they sensed their own lives depended on the outcome.

A glint of light caught Shane's eye, and it struck him as odd because it came from above the heads of the crowd. There was a figure up on the watchtower, he realized — a girl, clutching the railing as she watched them. If she was a guard, she didn't look the part. She wore a flowing robe. Her face was deathly pale. And the glint of gold . . .

Shane could swear the figure was wearing a crown.

It was all the distraction Maddox needed. He finally connected, smashing the morning star's spiked head into Shane's side. The impact sent him flying, and the crowd parted, leaving him to crash to the ground.

Maddox loomed over him, spitting a glob of blood into the dirt by Shane's head.

"Looks like our little Devourer bit off more than he could chew," he said darkly.

Shane dreamed he summoned a panda.

The animal wrapped him in its arms.

Shane was protected, and all the hurt just fell away.

He lay there in the dirt some time before anyone came to help him.

"My name is Viktor. I'm a healer," said the man who finally crouched at his side. "How do you feel?"

"I feel like I just got slammed with a great big spiked ball," Shane ground out. His side was on fire.

Viktor chuckled, the wrinkles around his eyes deepening. "That's a good sign, actually. I'd be worried if you felt otherwise. I'm going to make sure nothing's broken."

He ran his hands over Shane's tunic, pressing lightly against his side. Shane winced, but the healer breathed a sigh of relief. "No broken ribs. Let's remove your tunic and get you bandaged up."

Shane struggled to sit up. "No," he said. "I'm all right. Thanks for your help."

But he couldn't quite manage to stand on his own. The pain in his side flared when he tried lifting himself from the ground.

"The dirt is no place for pride, my king," the healer said in a low voice. "Please, let me help you."

Shane hesitated, then finally nodded. "Okay," he said. "But not out here."

The man offered him a hand up. Once on his feet, Shane found the pain more manageable. He could walk on his own, though slowly, and he shuffled after the healer.

Viktor's tent was white canvas, lighter than the greens and browns of most of the camp. It was large enough for two cots, a trunk of tools, a small bookshelf, and a larger rack of tonics, herbs, and powders – plus a furry gray animal a foot in length, with perky, rounded ears and a twitching pink nose, who crawled excitedly from surface to surface.

"Don't mind Josie," he said, smiling. "She's always happy for company."

"Possum?" Shane asked, slowly lowering himself onto a cot.

"Fairy possum, actually," Viktor answered. "Native to Stetriol. A natural bond. We grew up together."

The healer rummaged through the trunk for bandages while Shane, wincing, lifted his tunic over his head. He saw the man's eye drawn immediately to his chest. And little wonder: Where his tattoo used to be, Shane now had a strange scar, which wound its way down from his chest and across his stomach in a vague, waxy outline of a crocodile.

"You can see why I like to keep my shirt on," Shane said.

The healer was surprised . . . but Shane noticed he wasn't completely shocked. He didn't ask if it hurt, or how it had happened, or whether Shane had been able to summon Grahv since the tattoo had faded and warped.

"You've seen something like this before?" Shane asked.

Viktor rubbed his short gray beard. "Just once. I thought he was the only one."

"Who?" Shane asked. "Someone in the camp?"

"I can't say. He swore me to secrecy. . . . I've already said too much."

The man dabbed at Shane's side with a wet cloth. It stung where it came into contact with the angry little welts left behind from the morning star, and Shane sucked air through his teeth.

"I could command you," he said.

"I am loyal to my king and country. But I've sworn an oath as a healer."

"What are you doing here, then?" Shane said. He lifted his arms to allow the healer to wind a bandage around his torso. "Why not go home? Why join up with a militia if you're not a man of war?"

Viktor snorted. "Men of war are in short supply here. Have you seen this so-called militia in action? Most of them are children who don't know what to do with themselves. They all lost something in the war, and it's left them afraid to go home, or angry at the world, or desperate for purpose. If you ask me, the leader of this camp is taking advantage of that need in them." He tied off the bandage. "Regardless, the people here need healing, and I do my best to provide it."

"I have something that might help with that," Shane said, and he pulled a small object from a pouch on his belt.

Viktor gasped when Shane opened his palm to reveal a small mushroom that glowed an eerie purple in the low light of the tent.

"I've never seen anything like that!" exclaimed the healer. "Where –?"

"I've traveled far and wide. Found some interesting things. And when my tattoo started to change, I learned that eating these helped with some of the . . . stranger side effects."

"Side effects?" The healer looked stricken, and Josie hissed in agitation. "What sort of side effects?"

"Just trust me," Shane answered. "If someone in this camp is having any . . . skin issues . . ." He tapped his bandaged chest. "You want to give them this."

He smiled and handed over the glowing mushroom.

Viktor nodded. "Thank you," he said. Then, when Shane rose to leave, he placed a hand on Shane's shoulder. "I've been a healer for many years," he said. "In Stetriol. The bonding sickness . . . it plagued me my entire life." He smiled sadly. "Whatever ills the Bile brought us, it cured that sickness. I know we have you to thank for that."

Shane was so used to scorn and blame that he had no idea how to respond to the man's gratitude. He felt a tightness in his throat and settled on a quick nod before throwing on his tunic and ducking out of the tent.

He felt a little guilty for lying to the healer.

If there'd been another way, he'd have taken it. But Viktor was an honorable man, and Shane knew better than to try to come between an honorable man and his oath. It's what made Greencloaks so impossible to deal with, after all. *Compromise* wasn't in their vocabulary.

But honest people were easy to trick because they expected honesty in others. The healer had no reason to suspect that Shane would lie about the strange mushroom—the mushroom that, in truth, was perfectly edible but held no medicinal properties as far as Shane or Yumaris could discover.

Viktor would seek out whoever it was in the camp whose tattoo had changed in the way Shane's had. If Shane watched him, he'd give away the identity of the very person he'd been determined to protect.

If someone else had Shane's . . . affliction . . . he needed to know.

His eyes drifted upward, back to the watchtower that rose from the campground's barrier wall. No figure stood upon its parapet, but Shane could swear he felt eyes watching him from its dark interior, and he shuddered.

Shane dreamed he summoned a falcon.

Through its eyes, he saw the world spread out before him as if from a great height.

He was untouchable.

Shane was sparring on the training grounds when a cry sounded from near the gate.

"The raiders! The raiders return!"

The girl Shane had been facing threw her staff aside. All around them, people stopped what they were doing and turned toward the gates.

Shane gripped his own staff more tightly. If they were under attack, why would anyone do otherwise?

But the buzz that rippled through the crowd was a buzz of excitement and eager anticipation. The raiders weren't attackers—they were allies.

Shane fell in with the crowd making its way toward the entryway as the gate opened noisily.

"Clear a path," growled Maddox, and he stepped through the crowd, taking the opportunity to shove Shane aside. Shane caught himself, but not before he'd stumbled into a boy, who cast him a hostile look.

A small band of warriors appeared in the open gateway. Unlike most of the men and women of the camp, they each sported complete sets of Conqueror armor, black and red and silver, with gleaming weapons on their backs or hanging from their belts. With them were three warhorses dragging sleighs laden with boxes and canvas sacks.

Here, at last, were the true warriors. It was obvious just by looking at them.

There was a moment of utter silence as the armored band stepped across the threshold. Then a great clamor broke out as the people all around Shane lifted their voices.

"What news of Stetriol?" called out a woman.

"Do you bring weapons?" cried a man.

"We need grain!" said another.

"Quiet!" Maddox barked. "Quiet, now!" And though the crowd continued to grumble, no more shouts went up.

Shane scanned the five armored figures as they removed their helmets and saluted Maddox. Their bearing was disciplined, but Shane could see in their faces that they basked in the attention their appearance had generated. All except for one, a dark-skinned boy about Shane's age, tall but slight, who mimicked the movements of the others but scowled as he did so.

"It was a fantastic success, sir," one of them said to Maddox. Her black hair was braided long on one side and shaved down to her scalp on the other. She looked dangerous, Shane thought, even before he saw that her weapon of choice was a brutal two-handed sword she wore on her back. "We took three vessels for all they were worth."

"There's much more plunder down at the edge of the forest," another one added, an Amayan teenager with the barest wisp of a beard growing upon his freckled cheeks. "It was more than we could bring up at once, but we have the essentials with us."

They were pirates, Shane realized. This small band of Conquerors had been sent down to the coast to prey upon passing ships.

"Excellent." Maddox beamed. "Well done, all of you." He slapped the scowling boy on the shoulder. "See now, Karmo? I said you'd get the hang of this."

Karmo narrowed his eyes. "I suppose a person can get used to just about anything."

Karmo was the only one among them, Shane realized, who didn't appear to be carrying a weapon.

He did, however, wear a tight bandage around his left forearm.

Viktor had stepped to the forefront of the assembled crowd, his neatly trimmed beard and small stature a sharp contrast beside Maddox. While the general fawned over his elite band of pirates, the healer organized volunteers to unload the sleighs and begin sorting the goods. The people of the camp seemed to respect Viktor, and they hustled to do as he asked.

Shane made sure to volunteer, and he kept one eye on the raiders as he set to lifting boxes.

"There is news of Stetriol, I'm afraid," the woman warrior told Maddox. "It's been occupied."

"Occupied?" Maddox echoed.

"The Greencloaks have taken over," she explained, real hatred in her voice.

Shane almost dropped a box.

Maddox snorted. "It's almost better this way, Yeffa," he said. "We were expecting a fight when we took the castle. I'd much prefer that fight to be against those dogs. I'm sure you feel the same, 'Greenslayer.'" He flashed his broken teeth. "We'll restore our rightful ruler to the throne over their dead bodies."

Shane busied himself with his task, fairly certain he wasn't the rightful ruler Maddox had in mind. He looked up at the watchtower, but the mysterious figure had not returned.

"We'll be ready, sir. In the meantime . . ."

"In the meantime, every ship you overtake is a ship that can't supply our enemies. You'll return to your post in the morning."

Yeffa saluted.

By now Viktor had set aside a small cache of boxes, which Shane knew must be supplies for healing. "Karmo," the healer called out to the sullen young raider. "Help me get these to my tent, would you?"

This caught Yeffa's attention.

"I'll have Fito help you," she said.

The healer stopped mid-turn. "I asked Karmo."

Yeffa placed her fists against her hips. "And I don't like other people giving *my* people their assignments." She inclined her head toward the scruffy teenager. "What's wrong with Fito?"

"Think careful, now," Fito said, running a finger along the ax in his belt. "You don't want to go hurting my feelings."

"He's quite sensitive," added Yeffa.

For a moment the healer just stood there, his gaze moving between the raiders, whose spiked armor caught the light of the sun. Maddox looked on with amusement, and the entire crowd seemed to hold its breath even as everyone pretended not to be watching.

Finally Viktor threw back his shoulders and stared Fito down. "So you know the difference between saffron and safflower, do you?"

Fito squirmed a little.

"No? Well that's okay, though, because you can read the labels."

"Aw," Fito said. "You know I can't read nothin'."

The healer turned back to Yeffa with an expectant look.

She clucked her tongue. "Karmo. Help the man."

And there wasn't a doubt in Shane's mind: Karmo was the one he was looking for.

News of the Greencloak presence in Stetriol spread quickly, and Shane could sense the mood in camp turning sour. Most troubling was the fact that as people discussed the development, they tended to glare at him. He felt eyes on him wherever he went. Eyes and blame. It was clear who they held responsible for the outcome of the war.

The one person who didn't seem to have ill thoughts for Shane was Karmo — but only because he appeared lost in his own darker thoughts. Shane had watched the boy emerge from the healer's tent with a fresh bandage on his arm and the same scowl he'd worn since arriving. Rather than reuniting with the rest of the raiders, whose boisterous laughter could be heard from across the caldera, Karmo set to pitching in around the camp, delivering more of the goods they'd brought up from the coast.

The evening meal was especially spirited that night. The raiders had returned with salt and spices, and the cooks had made use of it, teasing new flavor out of the routine bowls of stew and soggy vegetables.

Shane ate in silence while all around him the Conquerors gathered into animated clusters and talked worriedly about the news of the day. Maddox's desire to take Stetriol from the Greencloaks had stirred up a lot of concern, but the fearful talk of those around Shane was all but drowned out by the raiders, who competed to speak over one another as they shared tales of their glory. In addition to the woman warrior from Nilo and the scruffy Amayan pirate, there were two young men who appeared to be Hundred Islanders. They both had swirling, wave-like tattoos upon their faces, and their features were so similar that they had to be brothers. Karmo sat among them, but he was mostly quiet, and he excused himself early.

As he stepped out from the canvas cover of the dining area, he scratched absently at the bandage on his arm.

Shane wasn't wholly surprised when Karmo made a break for it later that night.

The Niloan boy had paced the campground for hours, waiting for the raiders to turn in for the night. Shane was just gathering the courage to approach him when a cloud passed across the moon, deepening the darkness of the night, and Karmo slipped between two posts in the tall wooden wall and was gone.

Shane cursed under his breath and quickly but quietly dashed to the breach in the wall, squeezing through after him. If Karmo got too far ahead, Shane might never catch him.

But there was really only one direction Karmo could go. From the fort atop the mountain, it was all downhill to the ocean.

Shane moved as quickly as he dared, fearful of taking a wrong step that would send him tumbling down. He kept peering ahead, hoping to catch a glimpse of Karmo in the moonlight. He could hear the gentle shush of the ocean beyond the trees, and knew he was quickly running out of island.

Suddenly the hair on the back of Shane's neck rose. The air around him seemed to crackle.

And a body slammed into him from the trees to his side, tackling him to the ground.

Shane landed on his back. Karmo was on top of him, pinning him down and drawing back his fist.

"Wait!" Shane cried, holding up his hands, but Karmo's fist found his jaw and Shane saw stars.

"I said *wait*," he growled, and he shoved at Karmo. The Niloan boy tumbled back, slamming into a tree, and Shane scrabbled up to his feet. He raised his fists in a defensive stance.

From the ground, Karmo shook his head as if to clear it. "You're stronger than you look."

"And you're a poor listener," Shane said, but sensing the danger had passed, he unclenched his fists and massaged his aching jaw.

"I'm not going back there," Karmo said, standing, eyes boring into Shane.

"I agree," Shane said. "In fact, all day long I've been hoping I could convince you to leave with me. You've actually saved me a lot of trouble by running away."

Karmo raised one eyebrow. "Do I know you?"

"Probably," he said. "My name's Shane."

Now both Karmo's eyebrows kissed his hairline. "Shane as in Shane the Reptile King? Devourer Shane?"

"It's just Shane these days."

"Halt!" came a cry from above them. "Stay where you are!"

Karmo cursed. "We made too much noise."

"Can you outrun them?" Shane asked.

"Yes," Karmo said. "But we're on an island. They'd catch me before I could get a boat on the water."

"Okay," Shane said, and he felt the calm that always overtook him when he had a plan. "Hit me again."

"What?"

"Trust me," Shane said.

"Trust you, or hit you?" Karmo asked.

Shane grinned. "Little bit of both."

"I heard you were weird," Karmo said. But he shrugged, wound up, and punched Shane in the cheek.

It wasn't as strong a blow as before; Karmo was holding back. But Shane let the momentum of the punch send him backward, and he landed hard on the ground just as a pair of guards appeared, crashing through the trees.

"Fine, I give up!" Shane shouted. "I'll go back! You win, Karmo."

"What's going on here?" one of the guards asked. But he was asking Karmo, and his tone wasn't hostile or accusatory.

"I . . . caught this one sneaking away in the night," Karmo said, catching onto Shane's plan just in time.

"A deserter, huh?" the guard said.

"And look who it is," the other guard added. "I knew we shouldn't have given him a second chance."

"A traitor *and* a coward," the first guard said. "I didn't want to believe it."

Karmo swallowed. "Believe it," he said solemnly. "King Shane is a no-good snake."

"Well, this is a familiar and not unwelcome sight," Maddox said. The moonlight glinted off his bald head. "Though you surely must be tired of this view of my boots by now, your majesty."

"It's the *smell* of your boots that I could do without," Shane said. He'd been dragged back to the campsite and again forced to his knees before the self-proclaimed general. Karmo had come back, too, seemingly content to follow Shane's lead, but he couldn't be sure the boy wouldn't simply slip away again first chance he got.

"What are you up to?" Maddox demanded. "Spying on us? Who were you going to run to?"

Shane said nothing.

"Are you working with the Greencloaks?"

Shane gritted his teeth. He felt his face twitch at the accusation, but he remained silent.

"A few days in a cell should soften you up." Maddox turned to the guards. "Throw him in the Reptile House."

Once or twice in his time at the camp, Shane had caught a whiff of something unpleasant on the breeze. Now he knew where it had been coming from.

The Reptile House was one of the few true structures in the camp, built of wood and stone. Shane had pegged it as a dry storage space for foodstuffs, but the truth was much stranger.

Snakes. The structure was full of snakes. And lizards, and a tortoise, and even some toads, which Shane knew were not reptiles at all but amphibians.

The animals were kept behind glass, which was a luxury in this part of the world. The building was obviously meant to be a place where animals could be kept on display, like Stetriol's castle garden with its barred cages. But Shane knew those cells had held exotic birds and mammals from all across Stetriol. Who would want to keep so many smelly, scaly reptiles on display?

Shane had no way of measuring the time that passed. There were no windows. Neither was there anywhere comfortable to sit, but after hours of pacing the stone floor, his legs ached. He was locked behind a large glass panel as if on display, but no one came by, not to see him or taunt him or bring him food.

And snakes, he'd found, were poor company.

As the day dragged on, Shane felt weak and fuzzy. He stretched his aching muscles, but it was the lack of water that was getting to him more than anything else. He felt a buzzing in the air, felt his skin begin to tingle. And just when he thought he might be losing his mind, Karmo entered the Reptile House.

"I convinced them to let me talk to you first," he explained, slipping a bowl of water through a slot in the cell door. "Maddox figured you'd have it out for me, since I'm the one who dragged you back, and he thought you might let something slip in anger."

Shane drank deeply from the bowl, smacking his lips. "Maddox doesn't think highly enough of me."

"I'm coming around, though," Karmo said. "Why'd you throw yourself to the wolves to help me?"

"I suspect you're meant for greater things, Karmo. I don't think you're buying into whatever Maddox is selling. Tell me if I'm wrong."

Karmo sighed. "You're not wrong."

"So how'd you end up here?"

"Chasing the worst kind of trouble: good intentions."

Shane smiled. "I might know a thing or two about that."

"You know Zerif too, right? He's the one who dragged me into this mess."

The smile fell away from Shane's face.

"Yeah, that's what I thought," Karmo said. "The guy's real good at selling you on his plan, but then when things go south he's nowhere around. I was a Conqueror all of three minutes before I got thrown into a dungeon in Eura. And that's where I spent the whole war."

"Zerif had you hunting talismans?"

Karmo nodded. "Me and a group of kids that he called his 'special project.' He said it wasn't enough to conquer people through force; he wanted to conquer 'hearts and minds' too. So he bonded us to animals that people would recognize from old stories. We were supposed to be heroes. But the other kids he chose were anything but."

"You know what they say," Shane replied. "Fish of like scale swim together."

"That's the truth," said Karmo. "Zerif chose some real lowlifes. Devin was a bully. Ana was a thief. And Tahlia, the girl from Stetriol? She was downright vicious. We were all afraid of her."

"I knew her," Shane said, remembering the slight, blond girl whose spirit animal was the legendary water-holding frog of Stetriol. "She spent more time sharpening her knives than talking to people."

What Shane didn't say was that he'd seen the girl die many months ago with his own eyes, consumed by flames on a dock in Northern Eura. Though he'd won a talisman from the Greencloaks in that battle, the losses had been incredible . . . and painful. Faced with such devastation, Shane had decided that day that he would activate their secret asset in the next battle. Let the Greencloaks hurt one another for a change.

"That's her," Karmo said. "And there I was, just wanting to help my village. Do you know where Rain Dancers come from?"

Shane shook his head.

"Neither does anybody else. But there's an old legend that says they're chosen by the hammerkop – a weird-looking bird that supposedly has the ability to call down lightning." Karmo let out a loud breath. "My tribe has never had a Rain Dancer. That means we get less respect in Nilo than the insects and grubs. I thought having a hammerkop following me around would put us on the map."

"And instead you got locked up, disappearing when your people needed you most."

"Right. And by the time I made it back home, the Bile had worn off and my spirit animal was gone. All I had to show for it was a messed up tattoo that *almost* looked like a hammerkop. That didn't sit well with anybody. They exiled me." He considered his bandaged forearm for a moment. "I ended up here because I didn't have anywhere else to go. But combat training is mandatory, and Maddox put me on his elite crew when he realized how good I am in a fight.

"It would be one thing if they wanted me to guard this place and keep everybody safe. But they have me attacking ships, threatening innocent people, stealing from them. And they call me a hero for it." His eyes grew hard. "Finally getting called a hero, and it's for all the wrong reasons."

Shane sighed. "I try not to get too hung up on labels."

"Yeah, right," Karmo said. "But what are *you* doing here? I can only guess you didn't have many options."

"I'm here because something bad is coming. Something that's going to make Kovo and Gerathon look as scary as a couple of puppies." He cracked his knuckles. "I thought I might try to get in its way."

"You see a problem coming and you run *toward* it?" Karmo scoffed. "They were right about you. You're crazy."

Shane fixed him with a serious look. "There's no running away from this, Karmo. There's no place on Erdas people will be safe if what I fear comes to pass."

"Still doesn't explain why you'd come here."

"I needed an army," Shane answered. "I heard Maddox had put one together, and I figured I'd take it."

Karmo laughed. "You've got nerve all right. But I don't know if you've noticed: Maddox's militia is a bad joke."

"It's not a total loss if you come with me."

Karmo looked skeptical.

"I've been recruiting," Shane said. "I have allies – a team of people with special talents." He smirked. "I think you'd fit right in."

"It's got to be better than here," Karmo replied. "But we have to leave now, and this time, we have to be quiet about it. I can get the key off the guard if you're ready to run."

"I'm ready. I only wish I could see the look on Maddox's face when he realizes we're gone."

"Yeah." Karmo chuckled, turning to go. "His boss is going to be pretty upset with him."

"Wait," Shane said. "His boss? Isn't Maddox in charge here?"

"Maddox? You think that guy could put anything like this together? No way. He's just doing whatever *she* tells him to do. The Reptile Queen."

A chill ran down Shane's spine. "The Reptile Queen?"

"That's what she calls herself."

Shane felt a weight in the pit of his stomach, as if he'd swallowed a rock, heavy and sharp. It was the feeling he got whenever he realized something bad was happening – and that it was his fault.

"I can't leave," he said.

Karmo gave him a look.

"I can't sneak away in the night while someone calling herself by that name is planning to lead these people into a war they can't possibly win." Shane returned Karmo's look with a determined glare of his own. "She's got to be stopped."

Karmo rapped his knuckles on the glass of Shane's cage. "By you and what army? Looks pretty lonely in there."

"My allies aren't far. Most of them are camped out at a nearby island. If you can reach them and bring them back here, we can storm this place and put a stop to this insanity. Talk to Alix—he'll know what to do."

Karmo shook his head.

"If you leave now," Shane said, "you can be back with help by nightfall tomorrow."

"There's just one problem with that plan," Karmo said heavily.

"What?"

"They've decided you're too dangerous to live. You're going to be executed in the morning."

Shane dreamed he summoned a leopard.

Together they were fierce.

And fearless.

And he knew he had been forgiven for all he'd done wrong.

They came for him shortly after the sun rose.

"Put this on," one of the guards barked, and he tossed Shane a cloak.

A *green* cloak.

"You must be joking," Shane said.

The guards pointed their swords in a way that suggested they were not joking, and Shane reluctantly draped the green cloak over his shoulders.

The things I do for other people, he thought.

Karmo had tried to convince him to sneak away in the night. They could always come back with reinforcements, he'd argued. But Shane couldn't stand the thought of leaving these people. What if they'd already launched an attack on Stetriol by the time Shane could return?

How could he do nothing while someone calling herself the Reptile Queen led two hundred people to their doom?

Maddox was standing outside the Reptile House with a small company of armed guards, and he greeted Shane with a wide, broken smile.

"I see you got my gift," he said, rubbing the end of Shane's cloak between his fingers. "I'm glad. I didn't want you to catch a chill on your way to the gallows."

Shane glared. "I'm not sure the color suits me."

"Oh, I wouldn't say that," Maddox countered. "It brings out your eyes . . . and your treachery."

"Lie to these people all you want, Maddox." Shane gestured with his bound arms to the guards, who were probably the best the militia had to offer besides the raiders, but who looked undisciplined and poorly equipped. "But we both know I'm no Greencloak and I have nothing to do with their occupation of Stetriol."

Maddox sighed, draping a beefy arm around Shane's neck and leading him away from the Reptile House. The guards followed, but a pace or two back, and Maddox lowered his voice so that only Shane could hear.

"We both knew it would come to this, Shane. Our queen's claim to the throne of Stetriol is . . . a bit of a stretch, frankly. For that to go over well, it really does help if the royal line is dead. And you're the last of your family, aren't you?"

Shane pulled away from Maddox's grip angrily, but Maddox only laughed and continued walking. A poke in the back with a sword convinced Shane to keep pace.

"And now, of course, it's not just a matter of installing her upon a vacant throne," Maddox continued. "We have to go through the Greencloaks to get to that throne. With the enemy ahead of us, we can't risk having a snake bite us in the rear." Maddox leveled his gaze at Shane. "The snake is you, if it wasn't clear."

"And you're the rear end," Shane said. "Got it."

Maddox ignored the insult.

The camp was almost deserted at this early hour. Those men and women who were up and about snuck furtive glances as Shane was marched past them, then they quickly returned to their chores. Shane knew he wasn't popular here, but he didn't see any triumph in the eyes of those around him.

He craned his head around as they passed the white tent, hoping to spot Viktor. But the tent's flap was closed, and the healer was nowhere to be seen.

The gate was open and unguarded. They exited the campsite and made their way down the sloping path that led down to the coast. Before emerging from the forested area that separated beach from mountaintop, however, they executed a sharp turn, straying from the obvious path. They were circling the island now, even as they continued to descend.

Finally the trees fell away, and Shane saw their destination. It was a hidden cove, a crescent-shaped beach bordered by trees on one side and mountainous cliffs on the other. The cliffs rose from the water, one on the left and one on the right, nearly meeting at the middle so that only a small channel of seawater connected this secluded bay with the larger ocean.

There was a small wooden structure on the beach, like a hut built on stilts, and a long pier leading out over the water. A lookout tower high up on the cliffs would afford a view of the ocean for miles around, and probably also a view of the watchtower at the top of the mountain. This site could therefore be in constant communication with the caldera campground. It was the perfect setup for launching pirate attacks on ships that passed too close to the island, except for one odd detail.

A net had been strung across the channel, so that water could come and go with the tide, but no boat could pass from the bay to the ocean. Shane puzzled over its purpose. Was Maddox trying to keep someone out . . . or keep something in?

Karmo and the rest of the raiders stood upon the beach. It was too far to see whether they watched him with pity or satisfaction, interest or resignation.

But there was no missing the crazed excitement in the bearing of the girl who stood upon the pier. She wore a white mask, featureless except for eye slits, and a velvet purple shawl draped around the shoulders of her long white dress. Her arms were wrapped in golden bracelets in the shape of snakes, and on her head she wore a crown of gold and opals. Shane had once worn that crown, and his father before him, and his father's father, and Feliandor himself, who had cursed them all.

The Reptile Queen held out her arms, bidding them forward, and Maddox shoved Shane in the shoulder to get him moving again.

"King Shane," she said affectionately as he approached. "How good of you to support my claim to Stetriol's throne by dying gruesomely here today."

"No one has to die today," Shane said, keeping his voice level.

"As opposed to the last time I saw you?" the girl asked, her voice muffled somewhat by the mask. "A lot of people died that day on the docks. I didn't, of course . . . no thanks to you."

"I never would have left you behind," Shane said. "If I'd known you were alive . . . that you were okay . . ."

"Okay?" the girl shrilled, her veneer of politeness shattering. "Okay?! Do I look *okay* to you?" She tore her mask away and hurled it to the ground, revealing her face, which was waxy and pink with scars from fire.

Shane didn't flinch, and he didn't gawk. He held her eyes with his own.

"Tahlia," he said. "I'm sorry."

"Are you sorry for leaving me to die?" she asked him. "Or sorry that you have to look at the *ugly* consequences?"

"I'm sorry for all of it," Shane answered. "I'm sorry we went to war in the first place. Sorry you got dragged into it."

She shoved him, and with his hands still bound he stumbled, but didn't fall.

"Backward," she said. "You've got it all backward. Declaring war was the last thing you got right. And I'm ready to run with the ball you dropped."

She turned to address the raiders and Maddox's guards, who stood upon the beach in two separate groups. "Conquerors!" she cried. "Deposed King Shane has been sentenced to die for abandoning his people in their hour of need and siding with Stetriol's enemies."

Shane turned toward the beach too. "Listen to me!" he shouted. "The war is over – and that is a good thing! I can offer you new purpose, but –"

"Shut it!" Maddox barked, punching Shane in the stomach. The rest of his speech left his lungs in a rushed and choking wheeze.

"The method of his execution?" continued Tahlia. "Irony!"

"Irony?" Shane rasped.

"You set the girl with the water-producing toad on fire, you idiot," she hissed. "It's only fair that you end up food for the crocodiles." She lifted up her booted foot. "Devourer devoured." With one powerful kick, she sent him soaring off the edge of the pier.

Before he hit the water, Shane saw a long, dark shape looming below.

It was the punch to the stomach that saved his life.

Shane's first instinct on hitting the water was to gasp in a breath, but his lungs had seized up. He was spared pulling in two lungfuls of water. . . . But he still needed to breathe.

His hands were bound, tied with thick rope, but his legs · were free. He kicked, kicked for all he was worth, and breached the surface, pulling in air before his wet clothes dragged him down again.

A dark shape darted toward him. Shane saw it in his peripheral vision and rolled away as it shot past. He broke the surface once more and struggled to stay afloat.

Maddox held his blade out at the edge of the pier. No escape that way.

"Shane!" Karmo cried. Shane couldn't make out what was happening on the shore, though Karmo's voice carried over the water. "I can't get wet, I – Look out!"

Shane rolled again, and a massive crocodile snapped its jaws shut where he'd just been. Its lunge carried it past him, the length of its scaled body fully three times Shane's height. It swam off, but it would be back.

He knew a thing or two about crocodiles. The one that had just tried to snatch him was obviously of the saltwater variety – and crocs didn't come any bigger or meaner.

But they had a weakness. And Maddox had unknowingly given Shane just the tool he needed to exploit it.

Shane took a deep breath and dropped beneath the surface. The water was clear, and he was more likely to see the beast coming from down here. He twirled, kicking his feet so that he moved in a constant circle while he brought his hands to his mouth and pulled at the tight knot of rope with his teeth.

It started to give just as he saw the long, dark form of the croc come into view. It wasn't coming straight at him this time, but circling, closing the distance while attempting to get behind him.

As the rope pulled free in his teeth, he released a little bit of the air in his lungs. He would need to breathe soon, but if he kicked to the surface now, he'd be making himself too tempting a target.

Then he realized that was exactly what he needed to do.

Shane had to time this perfectly.

He kicked toward the surface, keeping the monster croc in his peripheral vision all the while. He saw the moment it decided to make its move, turning its snout in his direction and slashing its long and jagged tail through the water like a whip. It shot forward at tremendous speed, and as it neared him it opened its jaw to reveal uneven rows of vicious teeth.

The jaw of a crocodile was its most formidable weapon, and it was a thing to be feared. The force of a crocodile's bite could shatter bone, and there was no escaping its grip as it pulled its prey down, down into the depths to be drowned and eaten.

But there was a curious flaw in the system. The muscles of a crocodile's jaw were perfect for clamping down . . . but quite weak when it came to opening again.

Shane could use that.

He rolled once more to avoid the crocodile's bite, but this time he reached out as it passed. Even while terrified for his fingers, he wrapped his hands around the crocodile's open jaw and squeezed it shut.

The croc abandoned its lunge and began to thrash in protest, but Shane held on. He held on – and he slipped the rope that had bound his hands around the creature's snout.

The crocodile was far from harmless. As it thrashed about, Shane had to be careful to avoid its tail, which would strike with more impact than even Maddox could manage with a morning star.

But Shane effectively had the animal at his mercy now. He tightened his grip on the snout and pulled, kicking away from the pier and toward shore. Breaking the surface, he drew in a breath and let out a triumphant shout. As his feet found sand and he emerged from the depths with a conquered crocodile in his hands, he had never felt more deserving of the title of Reptile King.

But there were no cheers awaiting him on the beach, only the sounds of fighting. Karmo had turned on the raiders. He was pummeling Fito with his bare fists, dodging and weaving skillfully out of the way of the teen's ax. One of the tattooed islanders lay unconscious at their feet, while the second one stood at the edge of the tree line, pleading with a huge emu, apparently trying to convince his reluctant spirit animal to enter the fray. The sight was at once laughable and pitiful, as the emu stepped back from the young man, regal and defiant.

Yeffa kept her eyes on Karmo. She held her great sword aloft and circled, looking for an opening. Her movements reminded Shane instantly of the way the killer croc had circled him in the water.

The militiamen who had escorted Shane and Maddox to the cove stood to the side, watching the battle with awe, clearly out of their depth.

Maddox had expected Shane to try climbing the pier,

but reacted quickly when Shane emerged on the beach instead. He bore down on him, swinging his weapon. But Shane had taken his measure in their previous match, and he dodged easily, then thrust the crocodile's snout into Maddox's face . . . and let go.

Maddox screamed, dropping his weapon to wrap his hands around the animal's jaws before it could slip free of the loosening rope.

"Hold that for me, would you?" Shane said, and he ran past Maddox just as Karmo took Fito out with a blow to the chest that sent the young raider flying back. The hit was so impressive, Shane could almost swear he saw sparks fly from the impact.

"I've got this!" Karmo said as he ducked beneath Yeffa's swing. "Get Tahlia!"

Shane turned toward the pier, where Tahlia stood trembling with rage. She took a step back, then seemed to realize she had backed herself into a corner. She drew two knives from her sleeves and charged.

Shane met her halfway up the pier, grabbing her wrists and holding her back. The crown slipped from her head and clattered loudly at their feet.

"Give up, Tahlia!" he yelled in her face. "Your raiders are done, and the rest of these people won't fight for you."

"They'll fight to the death!" she screamed. "War is all we know!"

"You can know something better," Shane pleaded. He felt the heaviness of the wet bandages wrapped around his torso. "We all have scars, Tahlia. We have to try to heal as best we can."

Tahlia shrieked, and she slammed her forehead into Shane's. He fell back, releasing his grip on her wrists, and she lunged, slashing at his stomach.

Shane pivoted away, and she missed, swooping past him and over the edge of the pier.

His head throbbed. He heard someone calling his name from the beach, and turned to see that Karmo had vanquished the last of the raiders.

"Shane!" he cried. "Maddox took off."

Shane looked at where he'd left Maddox at the shoreline. The crocodile was gone, nowhere to be seen.

He whirled around to see Tahlia splashing on the surface of the water, gasping for breath.

"Tahlia," he said gravely. "Give me your hand."

He reached for her, but she still held a dagger in each hand, and she slashed at his open palm, forcing him to pull back.

"Tahlia!" he said more urgently. "The crocodile. Give me your hand!"

He reached for her again, and again she slashed. She wouldn't let go of the knives any more than she would let go of her hate.

He didn't see any regret in her eyes when the crocodile clamped down on her leg. She held on to that hate, glaring at him as she was pulled down beneath the surface, spurning the open hand he held out to her until he could no longer see any sign of her.

He stepped away from the edge of the pier and took up the mask and crown she'd left behind. He considered them sadly for a moment, then walked to the safety of the shore.

Karmo clapped him on the shoulder, and together they turned to face the militia. They all held their weapons up, but in their mismatched armor, expressions of shock and horror on their faces, they had never looked less ready for combat.

Shane swept his gaze across them, looking each of them in the eye, one at a time.

"Will you fight me?" he asked them. "Can you think of any good reason to keep fighting?"

"I can't," called a voice, and Viktor emerged from the tree line. With him was Abhay, the Zhongese youth who had betrayed his people, and a half dozen others from the camp. "We came to help you, King Shane. These people don't need any more blood on their hands." He took in the sight of the unconscious raiders, the crown in Shane's grip, and the sodden green cloak hanging from his shoulders. "Is it safe to assume you're in charge now?"

Shane slicked his wet bangs back. "No, Viktor. I'd suggest you put it to a vote, but . . . I think *you* might be in charge here."

Viktor startled. "Me? I'm no leader."

"You don't have a crown. Or a fancy title like *general*. But that doesn't mean you aren't a leader." Shane put his hand upon Victor's shoulder, and he raised his voice to ensure he'd be heard over the wind and waves. "I came here looking for an army. But I found something much more impressive. I found a *community*. A community that listens to you when you speak. So what do you have to say?"

"I say . . ." Viktor hesitated. He licked his lips. "I say put your weapons down." He turned to the soldiers. "No more weapons."

A man dropped his long sword into the sand. A woman tossed aside her mace. Then all together, the rest of them followed suit, and metal hit sand with a series of soft thumps.

"You have everything you need to build a home here, Viktor," Shane said.

The healer nodded. "A new home for those who need it. Sounds like the purpose we've been looking for all along." He turned back to the crowd. "The war is over!" he cried.

A great cheer went up, and the assembled men and women swarmed Viktor, shaking his hand and slapping his back as his spirit animal, Josie, appeared in a flash of light. The fairy possum leaped excitedly through the crowd from shoulder to shoulder.

"The war is over for *them*," Karmo said in Shane's ear. "What about us?"

"We're just getting started." Shane smiled. "But this time, we'll be fighting on the right side."

Nick Eliopulos is an editor of books for kids and teenagers. His short stories have appeared in Spirit Animals: *Tales of the Great Beasts* and *Stuck in the Middle: Seventeen Comics from an Unpleasant Age*. An avid fan of comics, games, and monster movies, he lives in Brooklyn with two fish named after characters from a soap opera.